COBA...

Richard Graves

The militant Emir of an Arab sheikdom has a frighteningly realistic scheme to kill key members of the U.S. government through the use of nuclear devices that don't have to be dropped from airplanes. In fact, the device that conveys the lethal dose of radioactive cobalt is probably in your pocket right now!

COBALT 60

RICHARD GRAVES

John Curley & Associates, Inc.
South Yarmouth, Ma.

Library of Congress Cataloging-in-Publication Data

Graves, Richard L.
  Cobalt 60 / Richard Graves.
    p.   cm.
  ISBN 1–55504–844–7.—ISBN 1–55504–845–5 (pbk. : lg. print)
  1. Large type books. I. Title. II. Title: Cobalt sixty.
[PS3557.R289C63   1989]
813'.54—dc19   88–7987
                                                             CIP

Copyright © 1975 by Richard Graves

Published in Large Print by arrangement with Stein & Day Publishers in the United States, and territories; Canada, the U.K. and British Commonwealth.

Distributed in Great Britain, Ireland and the Commonwealth by CHIVERS BOOK SALES LIMITED, Bath BA1 3HB, England.

Printed in Great Britain

For my wife,
Teru Marie Nakano Graves

CONTENTS

Wheresoever ye be, death will overtake you, although ye be in lofty towers.

The Koran, Chapter Four

PROLOGUE

From his vantage point in a new office building, Hamir took in the panorama.

Spreading northward across the vast open square below him, thousands and thousands of people milled about. Beyond the line of barricades at the far end of the square stood a raised wooden platform, painted white. Sunlight flashed from the blade of a large circular saw housed in the steel table that rested on the platform.

In the background a tower of stainless steel, the minaret of an enormous mosque, shimmered in the noonday sun like an onion-crowned ballistic missile. Somewhere beyond the eastern skyline, Hamir knew, stood the forests of oil derricks and the perpetually bobbing walking beams, spearing at the baked land.

Rapid-fire Arabic blared from the transistor perched on the desk beside him: "... a day of great portent of our beloved land and city of Al Hakeer. We are witness of this tumultuous event, as one with this assembly of fifty thousand. ..."

1

Hamir picked up his binoculars and scanned the horizon to the west. The great square of Al Hakeer fronted on its ancient harbor, where primitive dhows sidled up to the freighters. Up the coast, tankers anchored offshore sucked in rich black crude oil from the desert.

Through the haze over the Red Sea, he could make out the jagged profile of the Island of Ishbaad, the citadel, some three miles away. Nearer, cutting white slices in the blue gray water, a trio of gunboats headed shoreward.

Above the disembodied voice of the radio announcer came the heehaw of police horns. At the far end of the square the crowd parted and a caravan of armored cars and a panel truck crept toward the platform near the steel tower.

". . . for what reason is this event on this day? . . ." asked the commentator.

What, indeed? Hamir's instructions had been simple enough. Go to Al Hakeer, and find out why this tiny oil-rich land had mortgaged all its gold for cash to pile on top of the billions it collected each year from the sale of oil. He had some of the pieces of the puzzle, but the more he learned, the more he needed to find out.

As the caravan halted, armed soldiers

dismounted and took up positions near the platform. One of them went quickly to the truck and swung open its doors. From inside, other soldiers manhandled a figure in a white caftan, a man of about thirty. Through his binoculars, Hamir could make out a face contorted with terror, mouth and jaw working silently. The man's right arm was bound to what seemed to be a splint.

"... and why has this wretch been singled out from among all sinners?" The commentator's voice was pious. "Only Allah and His Emir al-Mazir al-Hakesch al-Saloud know the meanings of these things. ..."

The soldiers hauled the terrorized figure up the half-dozen steps to the top of the platform. The prisoner struggled frantically, twisting away from the circular saw.

"The crowd is chanting," said the radio voice excitedly. Hamir could hear it, too – the sound of fifty thousand voices carried through the insulated American-made windows of his office.

"... in ordinary circumstances this worthless camel's son would answer to the law of Allah in the dust of his prison," the radio advised. "But, indeed, this is not an ordinary occasion. Even now the mighty ships of the Al Hakeer navy are making their way. ..."

As Hamir watched, figures, one in a snowy

3

caftan, hurried from the gunboats into limousines waiting in line to drive the dignitaries the hundred yards or so to the platform.

"Our Beloved of Allah, Emir al-Mazir al-Hakesch al-Saloud, approaches. . . ."

The heavy rushing of jet engines drowned other sounds, as the squadron of F-4s swept northward, low over the square, rattling the windows.

Below Hamir the throng seemed to ripple like marsh grass in a breeze. Its cheering was a continuous wailing sound as the figure in white mounted the platform, robes billowing behind. At the top the figure turned to face the huge square as the sound reached a climax.

Hamir studied the emir through his glasses. He wore the traditional Arab kaffiyeh and dark spectacles. His face was strong, with high cheekbones and a nose less prominent than that of most Arabs. The jaw was square and broad under a close-cropped black beard.

The emir raised his arms high over his head as the cheering continued. Then he moved a few feet to a microphone clamped to the railing of the stand. The throng fell silent, as if by command.

For several seconds nothing happened.

Then a deep voice said, "There is no God but Allah. Allah's blessings be upon you."

The emir's voice was eerie, like cool water after the heat and hysteria of the masses' cheering.

"O, my beloved, we have gathered today to mark a point in our history when, at long last, steps can be taken toward the oneness of the universe for which we thirst."

The emir spoke extremely formal, rhetorical Arabic. The phrasing was portentous, his words seeming to carry a weight that wasn't in them. The Arab, thought Hamir, loves the music of his language. As the emir continued to speak – of Arab culture long ago, of the wizardry of mathematics and astronomy, the poetry of Omar – Hamir found himself caught up in the mystical spell. Sudden static from the radio brought him back to reality.

Shaking his head, he made some notes and then retrieved his binoculars for another look. The poor devil brought to the stand earlier cringed between two hulking guards at the back of the platform.

"Allah's retribution is harsh. So it was in the past. So it is now. So it will be. . . ."

The excitement of the crowd was almost tangible, even from Hamir's vantage point in his air-conditioned office.

5

"...and if the hand offend, so shall it be cut away...."

That was the cue. An officer threw a switch, and the saw began to spin, its razor-sharp teeth throwing off the sunlight like sparks. The crowd gasped as the guards lifted the prisoner between them and carried him forward. In an instant the huge men flattened the man's splinted arm to the steel saw table, the victim's body sagging in a near faint at the side. Remorselessly, they pushed the arm and board into the saw. It bit the victim just above the wrist. The spinning blade sprayed blood in all directions.

The emir stood watching, his face stoic, his eyes invisible. One of the guards held up the severed hand, still bound to its splint, and showed it to the crowd, which responded hysterically. An official, apparently a doctor, hurried forward to minister to the victim, now sprawled on the platform unconscious.

The emir raised his arms. "Allah's justice is harsh. But Allah is merciful –" As he paused, the crowd murmured its assent. "Therefore, this derelict soul has been selected to pay his price to Allah in the harshest way, but he is blessed, for now he shall have the finest medical attention the world can provide. He shall be made rich, he shall go forth to recite the blessings of

6

Allah. Ancient and modern, harsh and merciful, are as one."

Suddenly, the emir shrugged off his caftan and emerged in a uniform of British cut, ribbons resplendent over the left breast. "...But even the riches Allah has bestowed upon his people are not enough while Arabs remain threatened. The Zionist knife remains imbedded in our flank!" His voice rose to fever pitch, then became suddenly quiet, almost conspiratory.

"But, my beloved, is it not *American* bombs that kill our brethren? Is it not *American* money that arms and equips and feeds our enemies?"

"Aye! Aye!" the crowd shouted.

"Yes! The hand that made the steel of that knife, the hand that wields the blade and thrusts it at us –"

The crowd began to chant. "Vengeance! Vengeance!"

The emir held up his hands, and the crowd again grew hushed.

Slowly, he raised one arm high over his head, finger pointed at the sky. "When Ramadan commences, there shall be *vengeance!*" Down came the arm, finger stabbing toward the ground. "And the leaders of the oppressors shall sicken and die! This I predict for you, for Allah has given me *His* sign! He is the Master of the Day of Doom!"

The crowd's response was thunderous. Turning abruptly from the window, Hamir shut off the radio with apparent annoyance. He slumped down into his swivel chair and realized his hands were trembling. What the devil was *that* all about, he thought.

It was one thing to cope with the underfinanced schemes of Palestinian terrorists, quite another to confront oil millions that might – or might not – be aimed at terrorizing Americans.

Ramadan was sixty days away.

That same day the publishers of a small but influential architectural journal in Bonn, Germany, posted a letter to a key security agency in Washington, D.C.

Gentlemen:
Enclosed are copies of letters from the appropriate presiding officers granting permission to our Mr. Heinz Jaeger to undertake to photograph important historical chambers of the White House, Capitol, and Supreme Court while they are not in use. This work is part of our continuing "Great Rooms of History" project.

8

At the request of the aforementioned officers we also are enclosing personal data and a photograph and fingerprints of Mr. Jaeger for your routine security purposes. We are confident of your discretion in preventing public disclosure of this information, which could complicate Mr. Jaeger's task.

Sincerely, etc., etc.

PART ONE
Something For The Bank

1

Three days later Hamir stood across the street from an aging brick structure whose dusty windows bore an inscription in chipped gold leaf, "Grain Exchange & Merchants' Trust." Although he spent most of his working year in Beirut, this building was his home.

His appointment was at ten, sharp. Taking a deep breath, he moved across the light traffic typical of this rather depressed section of Washington, D.C. He entered through the weathered door with its original wrought-iron bars and stopped, to give the almost invisible glass eye in the far corner a chance to look him over. As he crossed the threadbare flowered carpeting, two men in tellers' cages watched him in stony silence.

At a wooden gate leading into the working area he paused. A buzzer signaled that it was unlocked. He went on, through a heavy door of aged wood, into the area beyond, filled with modern offices divided by glass partitions and row on row of metal and enameled cabinets, computer equipment, and electronic devices. The people at work on files and computer readouts paid no attention to Hamir as he made his way toward a door bearing the discreet label *Chairman*. He rapped twice.

The door swung open by itself.

"Come in, Hamir, come in." The voice came from an old, small man seated in a large leather chair behind the desk. Drawn drapes behind him suggested a window.

"Have a seat."

Hamir chose a chair across from the old man and sat down carefully, his small briefcase in his lap.

"You have a written report?"

"Yes." Hamir unzipped his case and handed a thick typewritten document across the desk.

"Summarize it for me verbally, please."

"Yes. First, there is the matter of the bonds."

"What about the bonds?"

"As you know, the State of Al Hakeer has marketed five hundred million dollars' worth of bonds, backed by their entire gold reserves. The gold, of course, is in escrow."

"We bought a lot of them. If they default, we get the bullion." The Chairman smiled grimly. "But why should they default? They pump twice that much in oil every year."

14

"Their oil is mortgaged, too."

The old man's eyes narrowed. "Why? What do they need the cash for?"

"Just so." Hamir smiled faintly. "An economist would say they borrow long to pay short. In other words, the dollars they repay in the future will have lost much of their value, while their gold will appreciate."

"I know that, but still, why pile up that much cash?" He nodded at the document next to him. "I'm hoping your report tells me."

Hamir cleared his throat. "That is only part of the story. The more answers I got, the more questions came up."

"Oh?"

"For example, they used the cash to buy hundreds of tons of very sophisticated equipment – large diesels, stainless steel tubing by the mile, stainless plate, chemical processing equipment –"

"What for?"

"I don't know."

The Chairman was mildly exasperated. "Material like that doesn't just evaporate. Couldn't you get a look at it?"

"Not exactly." Hamir felt perspiration forming on his upper lip.

"What's that supposed to mean?"

"The material – shiploads of it – was taken

15

to the Island of Ishbaad, three miles off the port of Al Hakeer, and there, as you say, it has evaporated."

The Chairman leaned back. "Couldn't you get onto the island?"

"Absolutely not. It is under the tightest security."

"Couldn't you see anything with your binoculars?"

Hamir shrugged. "Some oil-drilling towers of the most ordinary type. Nothing else."

"They *are* drilling for oil?"

"The geologists say there is none there. The island is an ancient limestone reef. Seismic studies made some years ago by American interests indicated it would be a waste of time to drill."

The Chairman pressed his fingertips together. "What's your assessment?"

"I think it should be looked into further. The Bank, after all, does have a large investment."

"Do you think this – what was his name? –"

"Emir al-Mazir al-Hakesch al-Soloud."

"Is up to no good on his secret island?"

"To be sure."

"Why?"

"First, he is an Arab nationalist, a mystic."

16

"They can be troublesome," the Chairman agreed.

"But, more important, he is a brilliant technician."

"In what field?"

"Aerodynamics and nuclear physics. He won honors and a doctorate at Cal Tech."

The Chairman frowned. "A mystic, you say?"

"It is an important consideration in the Arab world," Hamir replied. "It is as T.E. Lawrence described it – Arabs can be swung on a idea as on a cord. The other day I heard him make some dire predictions of Allah's vengeance. It was a speech to his people, but it was rebroadcast throughout the Middle East. He has their attention. Already they are calling him 'The Arrow of Allah.'"

"What was the prediction?"

"A prophecy of something devastating happening at Ramadan."

"That's a religious holiday, isn't it?"

"Exactly. It is to the Moslems what Tet is to the Vietnamese, and it's barely two months away."

The Chairman pursed his lips. "And if his prophecy comes true?

"Then the emir will be a force to be reckoned with."

The old man's eyes narrowed. "I don't like

17

the emir's combination of money, mysticism, and method. It's too much for comfort. It is possible, Hamir, that we will have to close the mystical emir's plant."

He touched an intercom switch and spoke again. "Two things – buy another twenty million Al Hakeer gold bonds, and contact Firebird, Incorporated. Set up a meeting. The principal's cover name is Wolfram. Hugo Wolfram."

2

The temperature was 111 degrees Fahrenheit. There was no shade.

At the bow of the small outboard motorboat Hamir sat stoically, clutching the gunwales. The name of this body of water was most appropriate, he thought. The Great Bitter Lake. A desert of water in the middle of an even hotter desert of sand. The belly of the Suez Canal.

At the stern, seemingly oblivious to the heat, an Egyptian soldier leaned against the steering lever of the motor. He had taken off his shoes for comfort. Hamir was tempted to do the same, but his dignity as a banker

18

precluded that. Besides, his insteps would be burned by the sun.

The movement of the boat crawling toward the partially submerged freighter ahead failed to stir even the slightest breeze. Hamir sighed. So this was where the Bank had located Firebird, Incorporated. He could see its ash-gray ensign with the flame-colored bird hanging from the mast like a scrap of drying laundry.

Seated in a folding chair under a huge red and white beach umbrella on the forecastle was a lean, bronzed figure clad only in a pair of khaki shorts. The man, his head crowned by tousled white hair, peered through a pair of binoculars in the direction of still another sunken vessel farther out in the lake.

Hugo Wolfram, thought Hamir.

The Egyptian soldier steered the smaller boat toward the midsection of the freighter, where its scuppers barely cleared the waterline. He turned off the engine and let the boat skim across the glassy surface under its own momentum. Just before it touched, the craft swerved to avoid head-on impact. Thrown off balance, Hamir grabbed the iron lip of the scuppers and held fast. Ducking under the rusting iron railing, he scrambled aboard.

The superstructure of the freighter had

once been painted white, but its immersion in the warm, acid water of the Great Bitter Lake had corroded the metal and paint to a scabrous orange. As Hamir crawled to an upright position, he had a glimpse through the clear water of the eroded side of the ship, which reached down to the bottom, perhaps thirty feet below.

He picked his way around heavy chains and coils of rusting cable toward the beach umbrella. The man in the folding chair gave no sign of having heard Hamir board and continued to watch the other wreck a quarter-mile away through his binoculars.

As Hamir approached, the man raised a hand in greeting. "Please sit down, Mr. Hamir. I'll only be a few minutes more."

The Lebanese sat down wearily on a large plastic canister in the shade of the umbrella.

"Help yourself to a beer. Down there." He gestured at a small cabinet on the deck beside him.

Hamir, his hands trembling from heat, opened the cabinet door and grasped an icy brown bottle. He held the cold glass against his forehead and cheeks and then uncapped it and took a long, slow swallow.

"Ah," he sighed, "that is *so* good. Thank you Mr. Wolfram. It *is* Wolfram, is it not?"

"Hmm."

Hamir looked out across the water to see if he could make out what Wolfram was studying through his binoculars, but the glare hurt his eyes. He looked down again at the cool image of his beer bottle and decided to wait until Wolfram was ready to talk.

"She's coming now."

"Who?"

"Juanita."

"I see no one."

"The line of bubbles on the surface." He pointed. "There!"

Hamir looked more carefully. Now he could see small blemishes, like dust. "Yes. And what is that?"

"Just a minute." Wolfram brought the glasses down.

The stream of bubbles edged closer and closer until they were next to the ship. Suddenly, with a great splash, a diver surfaced.

"A scuba diver!" exclaimed Hamir.

The diver scrambled over the scuppers through a gap cut in the ship's railings, unharnessed the heavy twin tanks, and flung aside the black hood and face mask. Water dripping from the equipment evaporated almost instantly on the hot metal of the deck.

"It's a woman!"

She was exceedingly handsome, Hamir

thought – not large, but lithe. A strong, deeply bronzed face with high cheekbones and crowned by jet black hair. Is she Arab? Hamir wondered. If so, she was one of the new wave of revolutionary women. But even among the revolutionaries, he knew of none who would be entrusted with this kind of man's work.

She moved quickly, gracefully, into the shade of the umbrella and sat down on another of the plastic canisters. With a faint smile she extended a hand to the Lebanese.

"I'm Juanita."

"Hamir." As he shook her hand, he found himself at a loss for words.

She smiled coolly and stood up to unzip her diving suit. "Is everything in order?" Wolfram asked.

"Perfect."

"Good." For the first time he turned to Hamir. "Now we'll show you what we're up to."

Hamir smiled lamely. "Of course."

Wolfram picked up a small wooden chest, unsnapped the fasteners, and opened it. Inside were two devices that looked like transistor radios. Wolfram switched one on. A needle on a gauge jumped. "Okay for number one." He did the same for the other. "Okay for number two." He pointed across the water at the sunken vessel he had been observing so keenly. "Watch."

He threw the switch. Half a second later there was a bright flash. Scraps of black flew into the air, as what had been a ship seemed to dissolve in a large cloud of white gas and steam. An instant later a compressive *thump* hit their ears.

"Now you see it, now you don't!" Wolfram was obviously delighted.

Waves spread from the cloud in widening rings of brass and silver that caught the sun's rays and fired them in all directions. A rainbow formed in water vapor, then faded quickly into the desert heat.

"Very impressive," murmured Hamir. "Soon the Suez will be free again."

"You're Lebanese, aren't you?" asked Wolfram.

"Yes." The sudden switch caught Hamir off guard. "Why?"

"They have marvelous oranges in Lebanon," said Wolfram.

"Oranges?" There was no response except a slight smile. Hamir decided to start over. "The Chairman asked me to brief you on Al Hakeer."

Wolfram stared into the distance. A shroud of white smoke still hung motionless over the place where the sunken ship had

23

been. Floating debris bobbed everywhere in the now still waters. "The Chairman," he muttered. "Fine fellow, the Chairman."

Juanita left them to go to her cabin.

"How can she stand the heat?" Hamir wondered aloud. "The temperature inside must be even worse."

"This is a modern cruiser, Mr. Hamir," said Wolfram. "We have air-conditioning. Martinis on the afterdeck when the sun goes down. Water sports and, of course," – he smiled – "fireworks."

"It certainly seemed a quick way to get rid of a sunken hulk."

"Not so quick as you'd think. It took us a week to place the charges correctly."

"I see."

"We used specially shaped ribbons of C4. Nearly a ton of explosives."

"And they pulverize the vessel," said Hamir. "Very efficient."

Wolfram frowned. "Not pulverize. They cut like a knife. The vessel was chopped into pieces, and the pieces sank. Tomorrow we'll go back to make sure there are no dangerous projections left."

Hamir was finding it difficult to pay attention in the numbing heat. "The sun," he said. "Can we –?"

24

Wolfram laughed. "Of course. Sorry. We'll go up to the bridge." He stood up slowly. "It's air-conditioned."

"Thank God!"

Wolfram led the way to the bridge ladder. As they climbed it, Hamir noticed deep, rusty pocks in the bulkhead beside it. Bullet marks, he thought, probably from the 1967 war.

As Wolfram had promised, the bridge was air-conditioned. Bullet-riddled windows had been covered with plywood, but there still was enough glass to give them a view over the lake toward the Sinai side.

"I rather like the idea of a ship that sails nowhere on a canal that goes nowhere," said Wolfram. When Hamir didn't respond, Wolfram sighed noisily and sat down on a metal chair. "All right, Mr. Hamir. Tell me about it."

Hamir's relief was evident. "You have heard of the emir of Al Hakeer?"

"Only enough to know that he's one of the current screwballs in a long line of the same." Wolfram motioned toward the Sinai. "It must be the dry heat. It slows the flow of blood to the brain."

"Screwball or not, the Bank has made a heavy commitment to the Al Hakeer gold bonds."

"Then the dry heat has gotten to the Chairman's brain. Nothing personal, Mr. Hamir, but an Arab's promise is a Westerner's poison."

"Among the Bedouin, perhaps. Treachery is an art form." Unconsciously he drew himself up. "I'm Hashemite, of course."

Wolfram ignored his comment. "If the Bank wants to make a risky investment, what's that to me?"

"But there is no risk." Hamir explained that the gold backing the bonds was held in escrow in Swiss banks, that if the bonds were defaulted the gold payoff would be at a dollar exchange rate far below the present value of gold on the international markets.

"So the Bank's investment wasn't risky." Wolfram raised his eyebrows. "But you haven't been sent to Firebird to announce that the Bank has made a prudent investment."

Hamir glanced around the bridge. In addition to the usual ship's gear, there were a draftsman's table covered with diagrams and an electronic calculator, a metal chair, a cot, some scattered clothing, and three trunks painted red with the word *Explosives* stenciled in yellow on them. "I see you live with your work."

"Fuses and triggering devices." Wolfram

leaned against the ship's wheel. "Destruction is an art, too, Mr. Hamir. My palette and brushes are in those trunks."

"You are the Rembrandt of demolition, I'm told."

Wolfram shrugged.

"We are worried about the emir of Al Hakeer. The Chairman believes we might have to close his plant."

Wolfram sat down on one of the red trunks. "The Chairman's views are invariably colored by what would be good for the Bank. Does he want to cash in the bonds?"

Hamir smiled grimly. "That occurred to me, too, except that *I* am the one who brought the matter to his attention." Hamir cleared his throat. "Frankly, Mr. Wolfram, I have only a *suspicion* that things are not right, that there may be trouble, that the emir has all the resources to make trouble."

"I'm not an oracle, Mr. Hamir. I'm a technician."

"Please." Hamir held a hand up. "It is my fault. Let me begin at the beginning."

As carefully as he could, he described for Wolfram what he had seen, what he knew about the Island of Ishbaad, and especially about the emir.

"He has, as the Chairman put it, a

27

dangerous mixture of money, mysticism, and method."

"I agree." Wolfram nodded slowly. "Obviously, you have to find out what he's up to. Contingent on that –"

"Exactly. And that's what the Chairman wants you to do."

"I'll need more details, maps of the island, charts of the water, security arrangements, and so on."

"That kind of information should be available."

"Good. We will want you to join us, of course."

"Me?"

Wolfram smiled. "We'll need someone fluent in Arabic, someone who has a general feel for the situation."

"But I am a banker."

"Aren't we all?"

3

The Moslem month of Rajab was nearly gone. Scarcely forty days to Ramadan. For their next meeting, Wolfram had selected the fashionable Red Sea resort of Hurdagah on the Egyptian coast, some 250 miles south of Suez.

West of the city rose the rock palisades marking the edge of the desert, the beginning of the Red Sea trench. In front of the city stretched the clear, tepid sea itself, filled with coral, swarming with rainbows of fish and other organisms.

All in all, thought Hamir as he made his way across the hotel mezzanine, if one must do these things, this is the ideal place. He had spent the previous day exploring, since none of the others to attend the meeting had contacted him.

He turned down a hallway with a door at the end. His only advisory had been a penciled note slipped under the door of his room this morning: "Mezzanine Room A 10 A.M." He approached the door with curiosity and trepidation, rapped with some authority, then entered.

The windowless room was illuminated by recessed fluorescent fixtures in the ceiling. There was a long table lined by comfortable upholstered chairs, all but one of them occupied. At the far end was a rostrum and a reflective screen. At the near end of the table was a projector. At each place by the table were two small thermos bottles, one for tea, one for Egyptian coffee, cups, and ruled pads and pencils. From the look of things, the meeting has been going on for some time.

"Please come in," said Wolfram, standing up. "This is Mr. Hamir, who will be associated with us in this venture. Mr. Hamir, allow me to introduce the others." He pointed to each. "Juanita you already have met. She is, as you know, our diver.

"Next to her is Mr. Kinsey. He is an authority on helicopters, as well as conventional aircraft.

"The distinguished Japanese gentleman across from Mr. Kinsey is well known in his native land as a leading interpreter of Kabuki roles. For that, of course, he uses a stage name, but to us he is Mr. Harada. He served with great honor in the Imperial Navy. Among other things, he is expert in the ways of tides and currents.

"Finally, our black colleague is Captain Magraw, who knows all there is to know about ships, propulsion systems, guidance systems, and so on."

Hamir acknowledged each introduction with a nod.

"Now then, friends," Wolfram began when Hamir was settled in his chair. "Our new colleague has been good enough to supply me with factual material on the problem at hand. Each of you has a copy of this material, which we will run through presently. Before we do that, however, I have asked Mr. Hamir to offer you an appraisal of Emir al-Mazir al-Hakesch al-Saloud, which may suggest to you some questions and/or answers we ought to pursue." He smiled at the Lebanese. "If you please."

Hamir was not unaccustomed to addressing committees on complex matters. Still, there was something a trifle unsettling about this particular gathering.

"Thank you, Mr. Wolfram," he began. "Let me get straight to the point." Rolling his eyes upward, he began reciting the words of the emir as he had heard them. After a few phrases, he stopped and looked around. "That, colleagues, is how the emir sounds. You have to understand Arabic to feel the full impact of what he said. He spoke a kind of Old Testament-Koran language, full of fury and portent, saying nothing specific.

"As you know, the emir has a superb scientific education and a virtually bottomless well of oil, *ergo*, money. But what does he *intend*? Is he merely the desert-crazed Arab with visions of holocaust, or is there some method in his madness?"

Hamir paused for emphasis and then went on. "I think it is the latter. He may be mad,

31

but if he is, it is the madness of a Hitler or a Stalin.

"His propagandists have turned him into the 'Arrow of Allah.' Naturally, that has a considerable mystique in this part of the world. But what kind of arrow?" Hamir shrugged casually. "A rocket or two with the appropriate range? The emir could personally supervise the building of such a thing.

"What would he arm it with? An atomic device?" Hamir looked around the table. "I mention these things only as possibilities.

"What is he doing? And what does he intend?" He shook his head. "We don't know. We ought to." Hamir resumed his chair.

Wolfram went to the rostrum. "Mr. Kinsey, if you please?"

The pilot switched on the projector and switched off the room lights. A map of an island appeared on the screen.

"This is Ishbaad, the citadel of Al Hakeer," said Wolfram, "three miles due west of the mainland port of Al Hakeer. At the north end we have an oil tank farm, connected to the mainland by an undersea pipeline. It serves as a reservoir for loading tankers that moor at the end of the two long piers you see running more or less toward the northwest. On the eastern side of the island, jetties protect a small mooring site.

"The waters around the island are very treacherous because of coral reefs. A narrow channel has been blasted into the shore at the mooring site, but only a gunboat-sized vessel can put in there. The emir has three gunboats, by the way.

"The island is about a mile long, north to south, and about half that, east to west." He pointed at a lozenge-shaped structure. "This is an abandoned fortress, built by the Turks centuries ago. Before that, Red Sea pirates used the same site. In both cases the coral reefs made the area virtually inaccessible by boat."

His hand moved back to the jetty side of the map. "These buildings are warehouse structures. The towerlike structures are supposed to look like oil derricks. Okay, Kinsey."

The lights came back on.

"That's about all we have," said Wolfram. "At least, that's all we can *see*." He picked up a paper from his file. "I am intrigued by what we *can't* see."

He read, "Item: the emir has purchased the equivalent of eleven miles of stainless steel nuclear-rated tubing in various diameters. It was delivered to the island and it has disappeared.

"Item: the emir has purchased stainless steel plate, special welding equipment, et cetera, by the ton. It, too, has been swallowed by the island.

"Item: the emir contracted for, and had built, a relatively sophisticated nitration plant. It then was disassembled, delivered to the island and –"

"Where did the stuff go?" Kinsey asked.

"Let me read you some information supplied by friends in the oil industry who checked this island out some years ago. 'In this region of Southern Arabia underlying crystalline material appears along the coast. At this island site, the material is overlaid with Nubian sandstone which, in turn, is overlaid by a thick mantle of alveolate limestone. No oil.'"

Wolfram put the paper down. "All of which means that the island is full of limestone caves. Does that suggest anything?"

"He's got some kind of underground factory going," Magraw volunteered.

Wolfram nodded. "I'd say so. I'd also say he is doing something nuclear, in view of the specifications of his stainless steel, and so on."

"It is troubling," said Harada. "Nuclear

34

potential and a leader of somewhat questionable stability. Suppose he's building a power plant, not a bomb?"

"I think it is safe to assume," Hamir responded, "that the emir, with a comfortable percentage of the world's oil reserves, does not feel obliged to build an atomic power generator."

"Suppose he *is* making a bomb?" said Magraw. "So is every other nation that can get the material together. It's not a violation of anything except common sense."

Kinsey addressed Hamir. "Is our man unbalanced enough to trigger a nuclear device in someone else's yard?"

"I do not think he would explode a nuclear device. He would be too concerned about reprisal."

Wolfram was listening carefully. "Only if we assume that the emir is not that crazy. What about a *covert* nuclear mission?"

Magraw shook his head slowly. "Insinuate an A-bomb in somewhere and trigger it, you mean? That's a tough trick."

"There are nuclear devices other than bombs, aren't there?"

On a sunlit terrace overlooking the Red Sea they continued their discussions over

35

supper. "Our problem remains –" Wolfram commented.

"The emir?"

"Not the emir. No, people, our problem is to find out more about what is being done on the island."

"What do you suggest?" asked Hamir.

"Why, that we go in, of course."

"There is much security," said Hamir. "To start with, three gunboats. Electronic security equipment, guards –"

"And," Kinsey interrupted, "there is the fact we wouldn't know where to go or what to look for in the dark, even if we got ashore without detection."

"Are there any more caveats before we proceed?" Wolfram looked around. "The answer is rather simple. If we can't be cunning and surreptitious about getting the information, we will have to be stupid and open about getting it."

"Explain," said Magraw.

"Of course. Captain Magraw will sail his vessel, complete with the Firebird team – augmented by our colleague, Mr. Hamir – straight into the harbor of Ishbaad and tie up at the dock."

Magraw stared at him. "The old brass balls caper, right?"

Wolfram glanced up quickly. "There *is* a

rationale." He smiled at them. "Look," he went on, "Firebird Corporation is in this part of the world on internationally sanctioned business. So, we take our ship down the Red Sea to pick up some supplies. After all, we can't get it through the canal, can we? That's why we're there in the first place, to help clear the canal." He looked out over the sea. "As we are returning northward up the Red Sea toward Suez, we have – sprocket trouble – the ship's engines. We put into the nearest mooring to check it out. The nearest mooring happens to be Ishbaad. Simple."

"Gunboats," muttered Kinsey.

Wolfram turned to Hamir. "Didn't your report say they patrol together?"

"That's correct."

"In that case, we time their schedule. When they are optimum distance away, we move in. Keep the island more or less between us and them."

"Coral reefs," said Harada.

"What about them, Magraw?"

"We have the best depth equipment. We'll need good charts, too. The ship is shallow draft."

"Trigger-happy guards," said Kinsey.

"That's a teaser. What about it, Hamir? Will they shoot first or take us prisoner?"

"Great care would have to be exercised,"

37

the Lebanese responded. "Absolutely no weapons may appear. As few people as possible should be visible. All must be completely serene, even in the face of machine guns."

That's the way we go, then. Serenely."

4

Of course it was neither simple nor serene.

The plan and its implementation were cataloged in Wolfram's mind under headings like "What we know," "What we hear," "What we think," each of which included information, speculation, possible precedures, and personnel responsibilities. If there were serious contradictions, equations that wouldn't work, or combinations that promised trouble, he nevertheless conveyed assurance that he knew exactly what he was doing.

The first priority was their ship, the *Squid*. The special problems of the mission were summarized on the large chart unrolled now before Wolfram, Magraw, and Harada.

"The question is, can we operate in these waters?" Wolfram pointed at the shoal markings, the notations of coral heads around the Island of Ishbaad.

Magraw, puffing a cigar, nodded. "With care, yes."

"The waters look treacherous."

"No doubt about it," Magraw agreed. "But, then, the emir's gunboats seem to operate reasonably well. We have some advantages over them." He looked around.

Wolfram laughed shortly. "Advantages? Our *Squid* makes eleven knots at top speed. What can those gunboats do? Thirty, forty?"

"Speed is not the issue," Harada said.

"Right," Magraw added. "As you know, when Firebird bought the *Squid,* you specified a minesweeper."

"Of course. But to work with underwater mines and demolitions, not to outrun gunboats."

"We don't have to outrun them. We can sail where they can't."

"Show me."

"Okay," said Magraw. "The *Squid* was built for the U.S. navy in 1943 as a minesweeper. Because mines are usually planted in canals, harbor entrances, or ship channels, they are designed with a very shallow draft. In harbor waters at high tide, for example, they will sometimes ride around a mined channel."

"What's that get us in a face-off with three gunboats?"

"On the high seas, nothing," said Magraw, "but in shoal waters we can go where they can't."

"It will mean," Harada observed, "the careful laying out of sonar buoys to mark shoals we can cross in case we are pursued. By clinging to shoal waters we can, if necessary, evade them until we put into a neutral port."

"The gunboats, as you noted, are designed for speed," said Magraw. "They draw a good bit more water than the *Squid*."

"Wouldn't we be better off getting a gunboat of our own?"

Harada answered him. "Whatever we might gain in speed and maneuverability, we would lose in credibility. *This* is a mine-sweeper already employed in Suez Canal operations. It is a totally credible fact. The sudden appearance of a sleek combat/patrol ship might stimulate questions we could not answer plausibly."

Wolfram nodded, said nothing.

"Then there are some structural advantages," Magraw went on.

"Such as?"

"Well, because it occasionally has to withstand underwater explosions, the *Squid* had a double hull, double planking, and narrowly spaced ribbing. We could, for example, scrape across a coral head that would tear open the thin skin of a gunboat."

"I still don't like the lack of speed. I suppose there's nothing we can do about that, is there?"

"Yes, there is," said Harada. "Design the operation so we don't have to run."

Wolfram glanced at him with faint exasperation and smiled. "All right, gentlemen, you've made your case. If we can't fit our tools to the mission, we'll fit the mission to the tools."

Equipment was another matter.

Until they had actually been on the island to gauge what they were up against, it was pointless to make decisions on what special gear might be required.

At the same time, Wolfram – after consultation with Juanita and Kinsey – was confident that they had every type of underwater equipment they might need, stored within a large, closed barge trailing in the wake of the minesweeper. On top of the barge was Kinsey's two-seat helicopter, lashed down and covered with tarpaulins.

The barge, in addition to being a landing pad for the helicopter, was a floating workshop for Juanita in placing charges for an underwater demolition project. A closed underwater well and ladder arrangement allowed her to leave or enter directly to her equipment area. Inside the closed space, assembled in neatly labeled bins, was Wolfram's large inventory of fuses, triggering devices, cable, primacord, and plastic explosives. The space had special air-conditioning and humidification, vital under the Arabian sun.

"What's the status of our diving gear?" Wolfram asked Juanita. The two of them and Kinsey stood on the deck at the stern of the minesweeper.

"We have four complete sets of scuba equipment and suits, plus some miscellaneous spare equipment, everything in good, operating condition."

Wolfram didn't doubt it. She was as meticulous about her equipment as he was about explosives, and for the same reason – survival.

"I want all of the air bottles filled to max," he said. "It's possible several of us will spend some time in the water."

"What about underwater housing? If we are unable to operate from the ship or land, we'll need a base."

Wolfram unrolled the chart of the Ishbaad

water. Kinsey and Juanita each held down a corner.

"You see these little islands?" He pointed at two land areas at the lower left corner of the map. "Hamir says they are small, rocky outcroppings of the reef, partially under-water at high tide. After we have gotten free from our – intrusion – I want you, Kinsey, to go up and get some pictures of the area." He shook his head. "You know, we really don't know what we're doing, and I don't like it."

Kinsey and Juanita looked at each other. It wasn't like Wolfram to admit ignorance. Information was the key to Wolfram's magic. Without facts it was possible he was more handicapped than the average man.

"We'll get the information, Hugo," Juanita said. "You'll have everything you need."

"Sure," he said quietly.

Later, Wolfram went to the cramped radio shack, hot as a steamroom despite the air-conditioning. In front of an array of electronic panels, Hamir stood, stripped to the waist, his torso streaming perspiration. He wore a set of heavy earphones and an expression of puzzlement and frustration.

Wolfram tapped him on the shoulder, and

he removed the thick rubber pads. Shaking his head as if to clear his senses, he held up a sweat-stained pad covered with scribbled notes.

"We should be getting close to Ishbaad. The radio signals are very strong."

"Correct," said Wolfram. "It's time for a meeting."

Hamir sighed. "My contribution will be an analysis of smoke."

"It's the best smoke we have."

Wolfram led the way to the cooler bridge, where the others already were assembled. Magraw was standing at the ship's helm, staring through the tinted glass at the smooth, breezeless sea. On the portside horizon were the sepia cliffs of the Arabian peninsula.

"Hamir is going to fill us in on the latest developments on the Arrow of Allah via Radio Hakeer, but before he does, I'll make the assignments." He turned to Magraw. "Are we on schedule?"

"We'll be by the Ishbaad channel just before dusk."

"Good." Wolfram pulled a small notebook from his shirt pocket. "First, we're on a look-see mission. Everyone is a recorder. See it. Remember it.

"Our story is that we've developed a clunk

in the engines. We don't think it is serious, but we don't want to be on the open sea at night with the chance of no power. So we have put into Ishbaad to straighten it out. We'll be on our way again in the morning.

"As we go into the channel, we'll do the sensible thing and anchor our barge just outside the jetty." He pointed at Juanita and Kinsey. "You two will stay concealed inside the barge. After dark, Juanita will make her dive. Take the night vision scope. Move along the shore in a northerly direction."

"What am I looking for?"

"Man-made features – pipe outfalls, pilings, bulkheads. You'll cross the oil pipeline itself. I want you to take a Geiger counter – the small one from bin seven. I'd like readings every hundred feet or so, but particularly around the construction features."

"What about me?" asked Kinsey.

"You stay on the barge, suited up. If Juanita needs some help, she'll come back and get you."

"Shouldn't I go with her? It's not safe to dive alone."

"Safe? What the hell you think we're doing here? Juanita will be in shallow water, so there should be no problem."

"Sharks," said Kinsey.

Wolfram glanced at him in exasperation. "All right, Juanita, take the electric prod with you. If a shark stops by, juice him.

"What I'm looking for," Wolfram continued, "is a relatively high radioactivity count somewhere. If the Arrow is doing something nuclear, then he has to have a water cooling system. That means a discharge pipe."

"Is the radioactivity dangerous in that case?" asked Harada.

"Shouldn't be, if it's a run-of-the-mine kind of thing," Wolfram answered. "The cooling is by heat exchangers, which filter out virtually all of the dangerous stuff. Still, there would be a higher count." He looked at Juanita. "Check that reference in the Geiger bin. If your count gets anywhere close to something dangerous, get the hell out."

Wolfram turned to Magraw. "You'll stay aboard ship, supposedly to fix our problem."

"They may not let me."

"In that case, you'll probably be with us. Keep your eyes open. Look, see, remember.

"Harada, your job is to study security. Pay special attention to electronic anti-intrusion equipment. Where are the guards? How are they armed?"

Harada nodded. Wolfram had utter

confidence in Harada's memory. This man, after all, could recite all of the lines of a score of English and French plays as well as more than that number of Kabuki dramas.

Hamir was an unknown quantity. Wolfram studied him for a moment. "Do you have a better than average memory?"

The Lebanese shrugged. "I don't know. Usually, I make notes."

"You won't be able to here."

"I'll try to remember."

"Excellent. I want you to read and memorize the words and location of every sign or notice that you see. You're the only one fluent in Arabic. Look particularly for warning signs – high voltage, radiation, explosives, mines, that kind of thing."

"Understood."

"Your assignment is critical. None of the rest of us can pick up that information."

"I will do my best."

"As for me," said Wolfram. "I'll be looking for terrain features, especially around the old fortress, if we get there. I'll be looking at equipment, if any is visible. But, remember – be casual about everything. No probing, no pressing. If any is done, I'll do it." He looked at each of them in turn. "Everything clear?"

They nodded.

"Fine. God only knows what kind of reception we'll get, but –" He nodded at Hamir. "Let's hear what the Arrow has been shooting at."

The Lebanese cleared his throat. After Wolfram's precise instructions he felt ill at ease making an analysis of fuzzy rhetoric. He glanced at his notes. "There is only one fact to report. In a news broadcast at 10 A.M. today it was announced that one of the emir's gunboats has been sent on a goodwill cruise."

"Well, that's one out of our hair," said Magraw. "Where's the ship going?"

"The announcement said only that it would make calls at ports on the west and east coasts of Africa and then cross the Atlantic."

"Fuel stops, most likely," said Magraw. "The Komar class ships don't have much range."

"What's the ultimate destination?" Wolfram asked.

"Freeport, the Bahamas,"

Wolfram rubbed his chin. "That would put it near the U.S. coast in a week or ten days from now. Before Ramadan, right?"

"Easily," said Magraw.

"Go on, Hamir."

"The remainder of the radio activity has seemed routine – hourly tapes of the emir,

48

readings from the Koran, taped excerpts from the public performance I witnessed."

Wolfram stared out at the sea. "So, his people continue to hear that the mystical arrows will pierce the villains. And a gunboat heads for the Bahamas." He turned back to them. "Significant?"

"What could one small gunboat do?" Hamir asked.

"The Komar's are equipped to fire missiles, aren't they, Magraw?"

"In Soviet service they're equipped with two launchers to handle the SSN-2A missile. That's the Styx."

"But SSNs have a range of only about twenty miles," said Wolfram. "And they carry conventional warheads, not nuclear."

"Beside," added Juanita, "we don't know if the Arrow has such weapons."

"Why not?" asked Magraw. "The Egyptians have had them for years. They sank an Israeli destroyer with one in 1967."

It's one of the things we'll have to find out," said Wolfram.

"Do you really think this madman might be planning a nuclear attack of some kind?" Juanita asked Wolfram.

"I don't have the faintest idea," he growled. "That's why we're on this outing, isn't it?"

"I'm only asking what you think, Hugo."

"Sorry," he said. "I just don't like guessing."

"Well, what do you think?" Kinsey pressed.

"I *think* the idea of a nuclear bomb is nonsense, but, then we're not dealing with a sensible situation, are we?"

"Give us a guess."

Wolfram turned to Hamir. "Let's have another review of the Arrow's words. When he makes his threats, where's the emphasis?"

The Lebanese fumbled with his notes. "The tapes have consistently repeated the part of the speech about 'arrows of vengeance,' and then 'a plague on sinners,' but stressing that 'the innocent shall be spared.'"

"Plague?"

Hamir read them the Arabic words. "He seems to mean a disease or poison."

"Bacteria warfare," murmured Harada.

Wolfram held up a hand. "But how could BW spare the innocent?"

"It doesn't," said Magraw, "unless the innocent are innoculated."

"It's a nasty idea, but it *can* fit, can't it? Harada, what do you think?"

"Relatively uncomplex technology," said

50

the Japanese. "Insidious. Compact. Easy to deliver."

"But what about all of what appears to be nuclear paraphernalia?"

"All the evidence is circumstantial," said Magraw.

"Hamir, what about it? Do the emir's words imply assassination?"

"I must say yes. No other word coincides so well with what he has been saying."

"But how?" Wolfram demanded. *"How?"*

PART TWO
The Isle Of Ishbaad

5

The two men stared down into the violet waters, their attention focused on what could have been a large cube of metallic bricks submerged in a deep pool.

"We gaze into the new dawn of the world." The emir's voice echoed in the vast, domed chamber.

"What is the source of this light?" asked his colleague. Both men wore long white laboratory coats stained lavender by the strange glow from the waters. Over his left breast, each wore a triangular device.

"The luminescence is caused by radiation from our nuclear reactor, Dr. Gamal." The emir pointed toward the bulky, ovenlike assembly on the bottom of the pool, its shape warped by the layer of water above.

"Not dangerous, I hope."

The emir touched the triangular device on the doctor's coat. "Your radiometer will tell you if our levels become excessive." He smiled. "Don't worry, doctor. The deep water screens the radioactivity from the pile completely. In fact, the luminescence is caused by beta rays absorbed by the water molecules. We physicists call it the Cerenkov effect."

The doctor stepped back. "Nevertheless, it is a little – disconcerting, this energy. It seems almost alive."

"In a way, it is, my dear doctor. To use one of your terms, there is a constant metabolism of elements, some building up, others breaking down, in a never-ending process. It is truly a reflection of Allah's presence in all things."

"Of course, of course." It was wiser to agree. Gamal was, in fact, a Palestinian and a Marxist, but in pursuit of the common cause, he was perfectly comfortable mouthing the day's prayers.

The emir led him through several ranks of leaded doors into a long green corridor. The bright illumination made them squint.

"You see, doctor," the emir continued as they walked. "I have found the root of inspiration by returning to the Koran. In it I find the truth required to pursue these important endeavors."

They reached an area that opened out into a broad, high chamber. The curved ceiling of the cave was clearly raw limestone. The concrete floor was subdivided by

56

prefabricated walls into workshops, drafting and engineering areas, and a computer room.

"Once again, Emir, I must congratulate you on this remarkable establishment," said Dr. Gamal. "It is extremely professional."

The emir bowed slightly. "I thank you, Dr. Gamal. As one scientist to another, I deem that the highest compliment."

"It was meant to be."

"The credit must go to Allah. I am merely his missile, his arrow."

"Of course."

"And your experiments, are they proceeding as planned?"

"After some erratic beginnings, I think we have accomplished our objective."

"Then the arrows of Allah will be ready to do their work at Ramadan?"

"Oh, yes."

"When will I have your report?"

"The report is ready now, but let me *show* you the results."

The emir was delighted, as the doctor knew he would be. As they left the large chamber, went down another corridor to an elevator, and descended in it to a still lower level, he thought about the kind of man the emir was. Brilliant, to be sure, a probable genius – but with a strange ambivalence. Here was a man, he thought, of extremely

57

advanced schooling in one of the most demanding scientific disciplines, who was at the same time a mystic with an almost unbelievably naive belief in the orthodoxies of his religion. It was as if the abstractions of physics and metaphysics were the same thing.

No matter, the doctor mused. The physicist emir had, indeed, developed a plan to set the whole world on its ear with a unique kind of terrorism. That was all that mattered.

They entered a waiting room, where the doctor removed a set of keys from his pocket and unlocked another door. He motioned to the emir, and silently they entered a dark hallway lined with windows overlooking rooms.

"Each of these windows is a one-way mirror," he explained.

They stopped in front of the first window. The tiny room on the other side was painted pale green, as were the rest of the cave chambers. Its only furnishings were a folding chair and a small table. On the table was a sheet of paper, a form of some kind. Beside it was what appeared to be a ball point pen.

"In a moment one of our subjects will enter."

A half-minute later one of the room's two

doors opened. A dark, thin man peered in cautiously.

"The subject's instructions are to go to the table, sign the form there, and then leave immediately by the other door."

The man went quickly to the table, picked up the pen, and scribbled a signature at the bottom of the page. Then he put the pen aside, walked to the other door, and departed.

"And *that* was enough time? Just passing through?"

The doctor nodded, looking at his stopwatch. "Some exposure began as soon as he entered the room. It took him three seconds to get to the desk, two to sign, and three more to leave the room."

"It is hard to believe –"

The doctor pointed toward the small table. "As you know, the pen is a cobalt alloy which we have treated to create cobalt 60 –"

"Extremely radioactive."

"Exactly. Our subject was exposed to more than three thousand roentgens of gamma radiation for eight seconds. Two of those seconds were in absolute proximity. He will, of course, be dead within a week of this moment."

They went on to the next window, which overlooked a larger, comfortably furnished room. Standing in the middle was the man who had handled the pen only a few moments before. He seemed none the worse for his exposure.

"As you so aptly postulated it, emir, the marvel of this weapon is the time span between cause and effect."

"He appears as if nothing has happened."

"True. Yet, he has been riddled by literally billions of infinitely small bullets. He is as mortally wounded as if they had been machine-gun bullets."

"When will the effects become apparent?" the emir asked.

"Come." The physician led him to still another window on the opposite side of the passageway. In that room was a man apparently asleep in a bed beside a great deal of medical equipment. "The subject here is asleep under heavy sedation. While awake he is the victim of nausea, vomiting, headache, and diarrhea. As you can see, he now also is suffering some early alopecia. His hair is falling out."

"Allah works in strange ways," murmured the emir.

"This subject's exposure was just six days

ago. The vector was the same instrument as employed today."

"Is it painful for me to do these things to my fellow man," said the emir, "but we are merely tools in the service of the divine will."

The left the window and walked to the next. "Here," Gamal went on in his clinical tone, "the subject already is comatose. There has been a dramatic decrease in both red and white blood cells. He is on the verge of death. He is sustained only on artificial devices. We are trying to determine how long we can keep the subject alive."

"That's what the Americans would do, isn't it?" asked the emir. "They would keep their leaders alive as long as they could with wires and pumps and false body fluids and electricity until even Allah would laugh at their futile efforts to cheat His messenger."

The emir's living quarters in the uppermost level of the cave complex were furnished in a western manner – shelves of books, most of them technical, comfortable furniture, and displays of simple but rare art objects. The only significant Arabian touch was a scattering of colorful rugs.

The emir sat in a swivel chair behind a broad rosewood desk. Dr. Gamal occupied a large leather chair. As he inhaled from his

61

Turkish cigarette, he thought how nice it would be to savor a Scotch. That was out of the question, he knew. Islamic law forbade hard liquors. He sighed.

"It was good of you to show me your reactor, Emir. In the few short weeks that I've been here, our work has been so compartmentalized that I was only superficially aware of what an enterprise this is."

"But worth it, no?"

"For the cause, absolutely." He puffed thoughtfully on his cigarette. "But, until today, I was aware only of the medical aspects – my own share."

"But you knew the souce of the cobalt, surely."

"I knew you were preparing it. I did not really appreciate that you had built a small nuclear reactor of your own." He leaned forward in his chair. "What you saw today were the actual effects of massive radiation. But your plan – I really have never heard you describe it."

The bearded man opened the drawer of his desk and removed a ball point like the one they had seen earlier. "My plan is simple, as unobtrusive as this humble instrument, a ball point pen. They are everywhere and anywhere."

"True."

"But this pen – or one like it – when treated in our reactor" – he turned the pen around in his hands – "writes a message of death. It becomes an arrow of Allah." The thought transfixed him.

"Yes," Gamal said dryly, "but what is the plan?"

The emir shrugged. "Simplicity itself. Our plan is to wipe out most, perhaps all, of the executive, congressional, and judicial leadership of the United States."

Gamal gasped. "But how?"

"You showed me yourself, just a while ago. They will be dead, and they won't know it – until it is too late. Our arrows of radiation will fall silently. They will kill slowly."

"Your plan's implementation?"

The emir twirled the harmless pen in his fingers. "We plant this – material – in all of the places where the U.S. leaders regularly gather. All we need is the briefest access to such places – and that is easy. One on the president's desk, or buried in the cushions of his limousine, in his bedroom, his toilet. How many seconds are enough for fatality, Gamal?"

"From a pen such as that, three or less."

"And so it would be with others – the Speaker of the House, the vice-president, the

63

cabinet officers, the members of the two houses."

The emir leaned forward eagerly. "You know, Gamal, I myself have toured the White House as a simple student in a party with others. I have been in many places where the president spends some time. *I* could have planted this material many times, and no one would have noticed." He held up the pen. "An hour, a day, a week later, the arrows will fall just the same. A month, a year later, they still will fall."

Gamal shook his head slowly. "Incredible! There has never been a terror weapon such as this!"

"Correct." The emir leaned back in his chair. "Don't you see the symbolism of this, Gamal? The unseen, implacable hand of the deity reaching through time and space to exact His will?"

"I do not have your vision, emir."

The emir recited, "In physics radioactive disintegration means the transformation of an unstable species of matter to a more stable species."

"So?"

"So," the emir said impatiently, "we apply this physical principle devised by Allah, to the human species, the American leadership. We convert them to death and divert their untouched peoples into the paths of righteousness –"

Suddenly, one of the emir's aides burst into the room.

"Well," snapped the emir, "what is it?"

"Sire, we have captured a vessel. There are prisoners, possibly Zionists."

"What are you talking about?"

The aide took a deep breath. "A vessel sailed into our harbor, directly to the dock. Immediately our guards were upon it." The aide glanced at a scribbled note on his pad. "The prisoners are a man who speaks Arabic of the name Hamir. There is a man of the Orient, a black man, and a Westerner, who is the leader. His name is Wolfram."

"Wolfram?" Gamal exclaimed. *"Hugo* Wolfram?"

6

Even though the sun had moved below the horizon, the desert heat still held the corrugated metal shed in a grip of hot iron. The prisoners sat motionless upon a huge wood crate in the middle of the building, their hands held flat against the tops of their sweating skulls. In a ring around them were a dozen nervous guards, each fondling a Soviet AK-47 with a full magazine and a safety catch switched to "off." It was clear that any sudden movement would lead to a sustained hail of bullets.

Despite their discomfort, however, things were going as planned. The minesweeper with its special barge in tow had approached the Isle of Ishbaad late in the afternoon without incident. The barge had been moored offshore with Juanita and Kinsey concealed inside.

Following the script, the minesweeper made straight for the dock precisely at sundown. While Wolfram and his team tied up the ship, there seemed to be no response on shore. Moments later three military reconnaissance cars with machine-gun mounts roared into sight and brought the four of them under their guns. There were shouts in Arabic, to which Hamir responded, demands for papers, some jostling from the guards, and finally, the parade to the oven they now occupied.

Through Hamir, there had been an interrogation of sorts. The officer in charge read their names from their passports – "Wohl-frame. Mahg-raw. Harrah-dah." He leafed through the documents carefully.

"Hah-meer." He studied the banker carefully. "Why are you here?"

"We have trouble with our ship, the engine."

"Are you Zionists?"

Hamir gasped dramatically. "Absolutely not."

"How do I know this?"

"Do we look like Zionists?"

The officer studied each of them in the dim illumination of the shed. Addressing Hamir again, he said, "Only *you* appear to be Zionist."

"I am Arab."

The officer was not convinced. "You must all remain prisoners until we find out who you are."

"May we speak to your commander?"

"That is impossible."

"Allah makes all things possible," Hamir said.

The officer's eyes narrowed. "Do not mock us. We are all devout here."

"I do not mock," Hamir said. "I only state a fact."

"Very well, but you must remain here until further word." He picked up their documents and walked out, leaving them seated on the crate, staring through the superheated atmosphere at the barrels of automatic rifles.

Each of them inspected the surroundings as casually as he could under the circumstances. The structure was about a hundred feet long by thirty feet wide. They sat facing ceiling-high racks containing inventories of stainless steel tubing, bundles of metal rods, and thick metal bars of various dimensions.

Along one wall closer to them was a tall pyramid of dull metal bricks, flanked by ranks of small steel drums.

"Those bricks," Magraw whispered to Wolfram.

"What about them?"

"They look like lead to me."

Wolfram glanced at them. "For radiation shields, maybe?"

"Maybe."

"What do the labels on those drums say?"

"I can't make them out."

"Ask Hamir."

Magraw leaned the other way and whispered the instruction to the Lebanese.

Hamir squinted. "The large print," he whispered, "says 'CO 250 KG.' I can't see the rest clearly."

Magraw passed the information along to Wolfram. "Mean anything?"

68

"CO is the chemical symbol for cobalt metal."

"What's is used for?"

"I'm not sure. Magnets, I think."

A guard snapped a sharp command. Hamir did not have to translate. They fell silent immediately.

Cobalt, Wolfram mused – what did he know of cobalt? Magnets – of that, at least, he was certain. He used cobalt alloy magnets often, to hold charges in place against steel structures. But what else? He tried to sort out jumbled thoughts about the properties of metals, but the random bits of information refused to form a recognizable pattern.

So, with the others, he sat in sweating silence to await the next effect of their intrusion into the Isle of Ishbaad.

That was the way Dr. Gamal found them twenty minutes later

A thousand yards away, Kinsey helped Juanita into her diving gear. The low-ceilinged interior of the barge was bathed in the red glow of the emergency lighting system. Wolfram had warned them against using the normal lighting, lest its more penetrating rays illuminate the water underneath the barge and create a glow that could be observed from shore.

"Ready?"

"Geiger counter."

"Right." He retrieved the device from its bin, switched it on. It clicked rhythmically, but slowly – the background radiation from the lights and electric motors. "I'm not sure how much good this will do."

"Why?"

"Water absorbs most radiation." He fiddled with the device and them switched it off. "I've set it to its most sensitive input. If there's anything at all, you should pick it up."

He handed her the electric prod. "Be very careful, *machacha.*"

"I'll be back before you know it."

Kinsey checked his watch. "If you're not back in one hour, I'm coming after you." He helped her over the iron door that sealed off the diving chimney. Carefully, he unclamped the brackets and swung the heavy door inward.

Juanita stepped over the rim of the bulkhead and grasped the ladder. Kinsey adjusted her face mask as she applied her breathing apparatus. He checked the gauges on her tanks and gave her a thumbs-up sign.

As she moved slowly down into the glittering red and black well, the wavelets plonked loudly inside the cylinder of steel.

The water closing over her mask and head left behind a froth of red bubbles. In a moment even they were gone.

If Wolfram was startled to see the pudgy shape of Dr. Gamal emerge from the darkness outside, he concealed it. He also complimented himself on his foresight in not attempting to use forged documents.

"Wolfram, my friend! So good to see you." Gamal moved toward them, hand outstretched.

With one eye on the guards, Wolfram stood slowly and accepted the Palestinian's handclasp.

"What on earth brings you to this Godforsaken rock?"

"I could ask you the same thing, doctor. At the moment my colleagues and I seem to be prisoners."

"Nonsense!" Gamal issued orders in Arabic, and the ring of guards backed away from their positions and left the shed. "You must excuse the emir's men. They're so eager to confront Zionists that they see them where none exist."

"Obviously."

Gamal glanced at the others. "The aide said something about a ship?"

"Yes." Wolfram replied. "Out starboard

71

diesel has been misbehaving." He recited their cover story in some detail. Their vessel was en route to Aden to pick up some special equipment when the engine began to malfunction. Rather than achor at sea, they had put into the nearest dock on their chart – the Isle of Ishbaad.

"But tell me, are you working on oil fires in this region?"

"Not right now," said Wolfram. "In fact, Firebird is under contract to clear wreckage from sections of the Suez Canal."

"With explosives?"

"Yes. I've worked out a technique using cutting charges to break up the wrecks." He clapped Gamal on the shoulder. "Remember cutting charges, doctor? You were my best student."

"I have enough trouble remembering my medicine." He turned to the others. "And these are your associates?"

Wolfram introduced them and then explained, "Several years ago, in Libya, I trained a group of Arab oil field workers in the techniques of demolition. Dr. Gamal here was their medical officer. I must confess, I had some concerns about training competitors to do what I do. Where are they now, doctor?"

"Scattered throughout the oil fields. In

72

much demand, of course. But, come, we must get you out of this damned oven."

"Marvelous! If we can get back to our ship we'll be out of your way until Captain Magraw has made whatever repairs are needed to the diesel. It's probably some maladjustment, nothing major. Will you join us then for dinner? Our fare is simple, but we'd appreciate your visit – especially under the circumstances." Wolfram leaned toward him confidentially. "I have several bottles of Scotch, if you're interested."

Gamal lowered his voice. "I'm interested, Hugo, but our emir is rather touchy on the subject of alcoholic beverages. I suggest you keep them out of sight until you're safely at sea." He spoke up again. "Besides, the emir has requested that you all join him for dinner. We have few visitors at our island and –"

"We don't look too presentable for dining with a prince."

"We'll take care of that. There are showers, and we'll lend you some robes."

"You're too kind."

"Shall we go then? Dinner is at nine."

"May Captain Magraw return to the ship to attend to his engines? We would like to get going again as soon as possible."

"Of course." Gamal called a guard and

instructed him to lead the black man back to the dock. "We don't want him to have a problem with someone who hasn't been briefed."

She swam through the dark, silent world of crenelated coral towers, sculptured walls, and grottoes, at a depth of thirty-five feet below the surface. The sharp red-filtered rays from her lantern would not penetrate to the surface.

The steep edge of the island allowed her to swim only fifty feet or so from the shoreline. To her right the coral walls dropped steeply into an abyss. Angelfish, wrasses, butterfly fish, Moorish idols, and doctorfish glided through the coral massifs and sea fans. Schools of smaller fish, flowing like quicksilver through the red beams of her lantern, turned this way and that in precise coordination.

Juanita kept a sharp lookout for sharks. Sharks never slept, she knew, and their remarkable sensory cells were better equipment than anything a diver might have to prowl the reef jungle. She held the electric prod firmly in her hand, the lantern in the other. The Geiger radiometer was hooked to her weighted belt. Attached to it was a plastic tablet and a black crayon.

The barge had been moored close to the point where the oil pipeline linked the mainland production areas with the Ishbaad storage tanks and depot, so it took her only a few minutes' swim to reach it. The thick tube, already encrusted with coral growths, seemed to crawl out of the black depths like some Triassic anaconda. The coral monuments had been blasted away to create a narrow channel for its path shoreward.

Keeping her light beam focused downward, she followed the line toward the island. As she approached the surface, she switched it off and then surfaced for a brief look, twenty feet from the jagged rocky face of the island itself.

There seemed to be no waves and practically no current. The pipeline rose sharply onto the land. About a hundred and fifty feet inland it abutted a brightly illuminated concrete block building – a pumping station, perhaps, or distribution complex.

Quickly, she slid back into the depths, lest the spotlights reflect from the surface of her diving mask. When her feet touched bottom, she again switched on the lantern, settled it against the pipeline, and turned on the Geiger counter.

Nothing.

She scribbled a note on her tablet and then moved on. The pipeline, she knew, touched the island's northeast corner. There the shoreline turned westward, continuing for about a quarter of a mile to a stubby peninsula. From the peninsula a viaduct carried oil lines from the storage tanks to the loading terminals a quarter-mile offshore.

She checked her watch. She would have time only to swim to that point, explore the viaduct, and then return before Kinsey would come searching for her. Fortunately, the swimming was fast here. A current close to shore pulled her along with it. As she traveled, her red beam searched the island wall for man-made features. There seemed to be none.

Midway along she stopped to take a reading. Again, nothing.

She paced herself carefully, moving powerfully, but not fast. As yet, she felt no fatigue. Unless she had to fight the current going back, she would make the round trip without great exertion.

It wasn't long before she came to the concrete pilings of the viaduct, where she stopped to make another reading. This time the needle on the meter fluttered faintly. She pushed from the sea floor. As she kicked toward the surface under the structure she

76

watched the meter on the radiometer. When she neared the top there was still more activity on the gauge.

To read the meter at the surface, she would need the light. If she used the light, she might be seen. She switched the lantern off and surfaced quietly, directly under the catwalk. In the distance, she heard footsteps coming slowly her way.

At the far end of the viaduct there was a pool of light – spotlights – illuminating the ship mooring. There also were navigational warning lights. Out there, on the surface, she could make her readings with ease, but she would have to make sure she was unobserved.

Conscious of time now, she swam rapidly along the line of pilings. Again she went down to thirty-five feet, to a depth she hoped would conceal her bubble trail. Once she had reached the terminus, she switched off her own light and pulled herself to the top on one of the pilings. Keeping well in the shadows, she studied the scene carefully.

Overhead she saw three lines of pipe – two thick black pipes and a thinner one of bright metal, either stainless steel or aluminum. The black lines continued straight into the terminus, but the shiny tube bent downward before that, straight into the water. She followed its line down to where it ended abruptly some fifteen feet below the surface, well below the low tide line.

When she reached her hand into the opening, it was pushed aside by a strong current of warm water. Clinging to the pipe, she again switched on the radiometer. The needle jumped completely to the right and stayed there. Juanita turned to Geiger counter knob to a much less sensitive level. Still the needle fluttered well to the right. She scribbled the reading on her plastic pad.

Her mission accomplished, she allowed herself to drift down into the blackness for her return.

7

"Gentlemen, the Isle of Ishbaad welcomes you." Dr. Gamal checked his watch. "We have thirty-five minutes before dinner. Since cocktails are out of the question, I suggest a tour instead."

The others nodded agreement. They had been led to one of the guard officer's quarters, mercifully air-conditioned, and were offered clean khakis from the military stores. While Gamal hovered nearby, they had showered and changed.

"One hesitates to return to the heat," Wolfram observed. The offer of a tour was a bonus, but it would not be prudent to indicate eagerness.

"It's not bad outside now," said Gamal. "The sun's down, and the heat dissipates rapidly. Besides, we're going in the emir's American-iced sedan." He smiled. "It was his idea."

"Lead on."

The limousine was just outside the door. They scurried into it like pedestrians fleeing a thunderstorm. The doctor signaled the driver to proceed. "We're driving north, Hugo. On your right out there are the lights of Al Hakeer."

"Looks like Atlantic City," said Wolfram.

Gamal chortled. "Odd you should remember that, Hugo."

"That you liked Atlantic City?"

Gamal explained to the others. "I took my medical degree at Columbia. My favorite relaxation was to go to Atlantic City. Somehow, it reminded me of home."

"And where is home, Dr. Gamal?" Harada asked politely.

"The Eastern Mediterranean." Gamal pointed at an illuminated structure. "The

79

control station for the pipeline from the mainland. It apportions the crude oil into the storage tanks that you see just beyond."

As the limousine glided past more than a dozen double tiers of huge silver tanks, Gamal said something to the driver, and the sedan stopped. "Those are the viaducts that carry the crude out to the ship terminals." Two of the long structures speared out into the dark sea. At the end of each was a spotlighted mooring site.

"I recognize the two oil lines," said Wolfram, "but what is the shiny line?"

Gamal hesitated a moment. "Those are water lines. Sometimes the ships need fresh water."

"I see."

"To your left," said Gamal, "is the old Turkish fortress, once an important bastion. But, as the coral reefs grew it became less and less important."

"Does the emir use it for anything?" asked Hamir.

"In a way, yes. Inside those thick walls, he has a small nitration plant."

"That's something up my alley," said Wolfram. "Can we see it?"

Gamal checked his watch. "Well, there is not a great deal of time."

"We'll make it quick, then."

Reluctantly, Gamal agreed.

They climbed out into the heat and walked the hundred yards or so to the fortress. A heavy chain-link gate barred the entrance. Powerful lights on long poles illuminated the walls.

"We'll have to look through the fence," said Gamal. "I don't have a key."

"What's it for?" asked Wolfram.

Again Gamal hesitated. "I'm not sure – fertilizer, I believe." He smiled. "Perhaps the emir can tell you about it."

"I was curious about that round stone structure," Wolfram said as they were about to return to the car. "It seems too short to be a battle tower, but it's obviously some kind of fortress structure."

"It is the old water cistern for the fortress."

The structure, about the diameter of a farm silo, seemed to grow like a leafless tree trunk from the coral shoreline.

"Does it still hold water? It seems rather small to serve a garrison."

"It goes well below the surface," said Gamal. "It's quite dry. You see, the Isle of Ishbaad is like a sponge. Limestone formations, mostly caves, rather too porous for water storage."

"So the Turks' water would drain away," Hamir volunteered.

"That's it," said Gamal. "Slowly, as if each soldier were drinking three times the allotment." He laughed. "It must have caused quite a bit of reprimanding of subordinates before they discovered what was really happening to their supply."

"But, for a short time," Wolfram pursued, "the cistern would retain most of the fluid. The seepage would be very slow."

"Of course. That's the joke, you see. The Turks thought the water was being pilfered when, in fact, the thirsty Isle of Ishbaad itself was taking their supplies."

Harada had been silent, looking around carefully while the others chatted. "Are the caves beneath the island useful? They at least would be cooler."

"The emir does have plans for the cave, I believe." He glanced again at his watch. "And speaking of the emir, we are due in his quarters in ten minutes."

Kinsey was working himself into his air tank harness when he heard a sharp rap at the iron door of the diving well.

He swung it open. "You had me worried," he said as he helped Juanita up the ladder and out of her equipment. The heavy twin tanks and lead belt clattered to the deck. She smiled half-heartedly as she pulled back the heavy black plastic hood and unzipped her tunic. Slumping wearily onto a wooden bench, she let Kinsey unstrap her swimming fins and toss them aside.

"Anything there?"

She nodded. "Viaducts carry hot water pipes out to sea. Radiation readings are high."

"Dangerous?"

"Just high."

"Good." He went to another part of the barge and returned in a moment with a thermos of coffee. "Any problems?" he asked as he handed her a cup.

"One inquisitive hammerhead. I sent him flying." She gestured at the electric prod lying on the deck. "It's beautiful down there, Kinsey. Frightening, though."

He nodded. "I'll give the signal to Magraw."

"If he's there."

Kinsey shrugged. "If he's not, he won't answer."

They had arranged a sonar communication system that could easily cover the short distance between the barge and the mine-sweeper. Kinsey triggered a series of Morse bleeps.

A moment later there was a return ping on his loudspeaker, followed by a recognition signal.

Tapping briskly, competently, Kinsey advised Magraw of Juanita's findings. Magraw responded that the rest of the plan was on schedule. Wolfram, Harada, and Hamir were to dine with the emir.

All was well – so far.

While on the Isle of Ishbaad, the emir spent his above-ground hours in a suite of rooms within the quarters of his senior guards officers. That was where Gamal took the visitors from the ship.

With mild apologies the physician ushered them through a security search by a stony-faced sergeant and into a lushly carpeted reception area furnished with divans covered in the finest Moroccan leather.

To the experienced eye of Hamir, the carpets clearly were rare vintage Arabians. But if the carpets were eighteenth-century or older, the art appointments most assuredly were late twentieth.

Wolfram and Harada instantly recognized the stark Mondrian patterns and metallic hues of intricate electronic circuit boards, displayed and illuminated like fine paintings. Scattered about in the room, bathed by spotlights, were wooden pedestals bearing gleaming machined metal components as intriguing as any sculptor's work. One oak stand held a dozen small tubular metal objects in vertical array, like a squad of toy soldiers.

"What a striking exhibit!" Harada observed.

Gamal was pleased. "The emir prides himself on bringing together the old and the new. Please relax and look around. The emir should be with us shortly. I'll inform him that you're here."

After Gamal left, Wolfram and Harada hurried over to the nearest electronic display.

"It's a sophisicated circuit. No doubt about that."

"I wish I could decipher these chicken scratchings," Harada muttered, examining the caption below the display.

"It looks like something more intricate than a cathode ray tube circuit, I'd say."

"This is very advanced work, Wolfram. I count at least twenty – no twenty-two – integrated circuits."

"Let's get Hamir over here to translate the label."

The Lebanese stood near the center of the

room, scrutinizing the arrangement of cylinders. "Learning anything?" he asked as they approached.

"Maybe," Wolfram replied. "But we need some translating done." He nodded at the objects Hamir was looking at. "What have we here?"

"Ball point pens." Hamir smiled. "Nothing more nor less – until one reads the label."

"Oh? What were they used for?"

"It is not what they *were* used for, but what they *might* be used for."

"What's the caption?"

"It speaks of death. It ends with lines from the Koran – about death."

"From a pen?"

Hamir was frowning. "It's a poem of sorts. Bear with me." He translated aloud:

These first-born
Of Allah's humble couriers,
Now harmless here,
When girded by the atom,
Will carry His message to the world:
      "Wheresoever ye be, death will
      Overtake you,
      Although you be in lofty towers."

"And *so* He shall!" a voice boomed behind them. "Welcome, gentlemen. Welcome to my house."

The three of them turned to meet Emir al-Mazir al-Hakesch al-Saloud.

Dinner was served at a large round table set up in the guards officers' mess. The tableware, a fine, solid sterling decorated with the emir's arms, was the only touch of elegance.

"Please forgive this informality, gentlemen," the emir said after Gamal had made the introduction. "Allah enjoins us to simplicity. And, then, one of the many lessons I learned as a student in Mr. Wolfram's country was the value of informality."

Wolfram studied the man. The emir wore a short-sleeved khaki military tunic without decoration and an Arab headdress. His beard was like steel wire, cropped short. His broad and prominent cheekbones created a mask for the eyes, which, at the moment, were black and unrevealing.

The meal was as uncomplicated as the decor – a rack of lamb with a side dish of mixed rice and chopped meat. They drank soda with ice. For dessert, there were trays of cheeses, figs, dates, cookies that clearly

87

were American imports, and rich coffee. They ate in silence, following strict Arab custom.

"Gamal tells me you met him in Libya," the emir said to Wolfram, when the dishes were cleared and they were drinking coffee.

"Yes, indeed!" Wolfram said, a bit too effusively. "Dr. Gamal was the medical director for a group of Arabian oil technicians that my company trained in oil well and fire-fighting demolitions."

"I'm most interested in your company. What is its name?"

"Firebird."

"You put fires out with explosives, isn't that so?"

"Just as you would extinguish a candle, except that for a candle the size of an oil well, one needs a very large gust of breath."

"And what explosive do you employ?"

"Most of the inexpensive types, since we use rather large quantities. I prefer dynamite because it is easy to handle, but occasionally we use straight nitroglycerin."

"That is treacherous, is it not?"

"All explosives are treacherous, Emir," Wolfram replied. "But, I'm sure you know that already in view of your very sophisticated nitration facility."

"You are observant, Mr. Wolfram."

"Dr. Gamal was kind enough to show us your establishment. Everything is most professional."

"Yes. Well, we do have our little cottage industries, Mr. Wolfram."

"I advised Mr. Wolfram that the plant was part of a fertilizer project, Emir," Gamal said hastily. I'm not certain that is correct."

The emir laughed shortly. *"Fertilizer!"* he clapped Wolfram on the arm. "My dear Wolfram, did you buy that?"

"I accepted it, emir."

"But what will your colleagues think of us? Mr. Harada, Mr Hamir, what do you think of this notion of making fertilizer for a desert where there is no water?

They said nothing. The emir picked up a date and chewed it thoughtfully.

"You see, gentlemen, my small emirate has been challenged by Allah to show itself worthy. We occupy space in the twentieth century, but we live in the thirteenth. Allah has given us many missions." He raised his hands and slowly brought his palms together. "One of my missions is to close the gap between the centuries. To do that, Allah has been kind to us. He has given us oil, and oil translates into money. Money into education and material. But" – he raised a finger –

89

"Allah in his wisdom has given us too little time."

"I heard your great speech, Emir" Hamir interjected. "There, too you spoke of time, a deadline."

The emir stared at him for a moment. "There is much to do."

A silence fell over the table.

Wolfram broke it. "About education, Emir – how have you closed this gap between the centuries? How can you accelerate the time required?"

"It *is* a problem. But" – his eyes widened – "we have learned much from the True Word of Allah and – from the Americans."

"Oh?"

"To be sure." The emir laughed abruptly. "You have heard that a child must crawl before it can walk and walk before it can run?"

"Of course."

"It's a lie," the emir said softly. "I train my people to build *missiles* before they make rifles."

"What type of missile, Emir?" Harada asked politely.

"Styx-type. Our Soviet friends gave us several when we purchased our gunboats from them. I personally disassembled these, charted the circuitry, blueprinted the components. Then," he said proudly, "I made an instruction program – with Allah's guidance – and trained men to make copies. We have built them all. And that, Mr Wolfram, is why we have a nitration plant."

"To manufacture your own solid missile fuels and warheads."

"Exactly."

"I'm impressed."

"My objectives are simple. First, we need missiles to protect ourselves from the Zionists and, eventually, to carry the struggle to them. Second, a work force that can manufacture a missile weapons system from start to finish can make anything."

"True," Wolfram conceded. "But where do you do all this work? Surely not on the Isle of Ishbaad."

The emir looked apologetic. "The answer, I'm afraid, is a classified matter."

"I understand." He grinned. "Perhaps I should keep a lookout for a gaseous diffusion plant. With your skills you'll be building an atomic device next. Or have you?"

The emir's eyes narrowed a moment and then relaxed. "You joke, Mr. Wolfram. If you are talking about atomic bombs, they are strategic weapons for superpowers. Massive retaliation, that sort of thing. For the rest of us, they're the stuff of fiction."

"I'm glad to hear you say that, Emir. You are one of the few men in the Arab cause with the capability and finances to build one."

"*Never!*" The emir lowered his voice immediately. "Not a bomb. Massive, random destruction makes no sense. It is an affront to Allah. It destroys the innocent and their works. Besides, there are more effective tactics for striking at our enemies."

"Such as?"

"Terrorism."

"It strikes the innocent, too."

"Sometimes, to be sure. But if properly employed against specific selected individuals – enemy leaders and the like – it is the most effective political weapon of them all, and, in the long run, the least destructive."

"But surely," Harada interjected, "terrorism is outside the conventions of civilized behavior."

"Really?" The emir raised an eyebrow. "The list of former terrorists who sat in the highest councils of 'civilized' governments is long. And most of those governments themselves are the children of terriorism. Not the least of them is the Zionist enclave, Israel."

"Among the dispossessed," Gamal said

bitterly, "all weapons are acceptable, for they are the victims of what you, Wolfram, Mr. Harada, Mr. Hamir, would call civilization. They owe it nothing."

"Perhaps," said Wolfram. "But, Emir, where does your modern technology fit into this pattern of deliberate chaos? Technology is the very essence of order, isn't it? There is no technology with chaos. Look at the Dark Ages, a time of chaos and terror – and an enormous attrition of technology, civilization."

The emir laughed. "Are civilization and technology the same *now?* What Europeans call the Dark ages corresponded with the time the Arab empire flourished. And all of your modern technology is rooted in the mathematics of the Arab – the concept of zero."

"Your own technology *is* extraordinary." Wolfram agreed. "My colleagues and I are intrigued by your exhibits in the reception room. Unfortunately, I don't read Arabic, so I'm not certain what I saw."

"You saw some very advanced electric circuitry, of course. Missile guidance systems, to be precise."

"And the metal components were –?"

"Rocket exhaust ports, housing of various kinds. All made of high temperature alloys."

"We saw a number of containers of cobalt while we were guests in your warehouse. Do you use it in high temperature alloys?"

"My apologies for your inconvenience, gentlemen. But, to answer your question – yes, we use a good bit of cobalt in high temperature alloys – and for other purposes. In fact –"

"Many metals are used," Gamal interrupted. "Many."

Wolfram sensed Gamal's annoyance, and wondered about it. "Do you employ cobalt magnets?" he pursued.

"Absolutely," the emir said. Again the eyebrows arched. "Are you interested in metallurgy, Mr. Wolfram?"

"I use cobalt magnets in my own work," Wolfram explained. "I don't really know much about the metals."

"It's a facinating element –"

"One of many," Gamal interrupted again. "There are the rare earths, platinum, titanium. Many, many elements with intriguing properties."

The emir ignored Gamal. "Do you know German, Mr. Wolfram?"

"Some. Mr. Harada is our linguist."

"Then he knows that the German word for a goblin is *kobold.*"

"I was unaware of it," said Harada.

94

"Long ago German miners were troubled by a certain ore, which they called the demon of the mines, the goblin – hence, *kobold*. From it comes the word for the element cobalt, which was the troublesome ore.

"'Demon of the mines,'" Harada repeated. "Sounds ominous."

"And so it is," the emir went on, warming to the conversation. "Are you interested in numerology, gentlemen?"

"I am," said Hamir. "I'm a banker, you know."

"Of course." The emir pursed his lips. "We physicists live in a universe of numbers – galaxies of them, infinities. Did you know, for example, that the infinity of even numbers is greater than the infinity of odd numbers? And each element, wherever it is in the universe, has its governing numbers? Cobalt, for example, is fifty-eight point nine, but it –"

"Emir!" Gamal said sharply. "You asked me to remind you of the time."

The Arab prince seemed startled. After an uncomfortable pause, he said, "Thank you, Gamal. Quite right. I have talked too much."

Abruptly, he rose. The others stood, too.

"Forgive me, gentlemen, but I have a number of things I must see to."

"Before you leave us, Emir," Hamir said, "perhaps you could explain a riddle for us."

"Riddle?"

"When you greeted us I was attempting to translate lines from the Holy Word. A caption on one of the exhibits."

"What is your question?"

"How did those lines relate to the display of pens?"

The emir smiled. "Perhaps to tell us that pens can convey many messages in many ways."

Wolfram responded. "Words don't kill, Emir. We already have such things as letter bombs. Why not a letter-writing bomb?"

The emir stared at him. "We must learn, Gamal, from our explosive friend Wolfram. He gives us answers to questions that haven't been asked."

"Accept them along with my thanks for your hospitality, Emir," Wolfram said with a slight bow.

"Allah be with you," said the emir, turning to leave.

At the door to his quarters he faced them again.

"Mr. Hamir," he said, "even in a world of superpowers and missiles, the pen is mightier than the sword."

They stood around the table in awkward silence. Finally, Gamal looked at his watch. "Shall we?"

"Will you join us aboard ship for a drink?" Wolfram asked.

Gamal smiled. "I dare not. But I'll escort you back."

"Excellent."

As they pushed their chairs aside and moved away from the table, Hamir engaged Gamal in a conversation in Arabic. Wolfram beckoned to Harada. When the Japanese joined him, Wolfram whispered, "I want some of those pens."

Harada chuckled, disguising his serious response. "You think they mean something?"

Wolfram smiled affably. They had played this game often. "They're booby traps, probably. I've seen pen bombs before. But if the emir plans to distribute them wholesale, we want to know."

"Exactly," Harada laughed, clapping him on the shoulder. "You keep Gamal distracted as we go back out."

Wolfram moved ahead to join Gamal and Hamir as they strolled through the entry leading to the reception area.

"Dr. Gamal, I have a question."

"Yes?"

Wolfram took him by the elbow and steered him toward one of the wall exhibits. "This circuit intrigues me."

"I'm the wrong man, Wolfram." Gamal started to turn toward the others.

"Perhaps not, perhaps not," Wolfram went on. "This is a medical question."

Hamir, puzzled, looked from one to the other. Then he noticed Harada moving toward the illuminated exhibit of pens.

"Really, Wolfram," Gamal was saying, "I am a babe in the woods about this electronic business. Put me with some radiology experts and I can talk shop, but I can't do a dissection on one of their machines."

From the corner of his eye, Hamir saw Harada's hand cover one of the pens and wiggle it free from its fixture. Suddenly realizing what was going on, Hamir interposed his body between the two men by the wall and the pen display.

"You baffle me, Wolfram." Gamal was growing impatient. "Now, if these circuits are like entrails, as you say, they would do the job of entrails. They do not. They do the job of nerves." Again he started to turn.

This time Hamir pointed at another display. "That one, Doctor – is it, too, a kind of nervous system?"

Gamal stared at him. "You read Arabic

as well as I. The caption can tell you more than I."

"I don't understand this poetry in captions," Hamir said, frowning. He pointed at the words. "See?"

Gamal leaned to look at the writing. "This isn't poetry."

"You're sure?"

Gamal looked again. "Of course, I'm sure. It's perfectly clear."

"But what *does* it say?" Harada asked, looking over Hamir's shoulder.

Hamir sighed faintly and looked at Wolfram, whose face registered no response.

Gamal straightened up. "This poetry business is confusing. I have to confess I hadn't really looked at these exhibits before. Perhaps we had better re-read the label on the pens."

"We've imposed on you enough, Doctor," Wolfram said smoothly. "Let's go to the ship. I've had enough deciphering for one night."

"As you wish."

As they entered the security area, the sergeant rose to search them.

"Perhaps he thinks we have some of the emir's cutlery," Wolfram chuckled.

"Nonsense," snapped Gamal. He waved

the sergeant away. "Going in is one thing. Going out is another."

Outside, the day's heat had dissipated and the dry air was almost cool. They elected to walk back to the dock area, rather than ride in the limousine. As they strolled, Wolfram and Gamal talked over old times.

"Something you said inside reminded me that you have post-doctoral training in radiology."

"How do you know that?"

"You told me. During the training program I ran in Libya, remember?"

"That? I enjoyed those days, Wolfram." He laughed. "You know, you're very good with explosives. One would never realize how intricate that work can be until one gets into it."

"But what about you? Why does a trained radiologist waste his special skills being the house doctor in remote places like Libya and Ishbaad?"

Gamal shrugged. "It's unimportant."

Wolfram didn't believe him.

8

Eleven days to Ramadan.

"We still don't know what the emir's up to." Wolfram held up one of the strange pens. "But, for some reason, I suspect it may have something to do with *this.*"

"You think the emir's parting word was something more than weak humor?" asked Harada.

"I do."

"So do I," said Hamir. "This man had no sense of humor. Then, too, there is Gamal."

"What about Gamal?" asked Magraw.

"I recognized him from dossier photos. He is a leader of one of the Palestinian terror organisations, one of the worst."

"*Former* leader," Wolfram corrected. "It wasn't coincidence that Firebird was retained to train his people. When they went on their missions they might as well have worn badges."

Magraw returned to the subject. "Where do we go from here?"

"That was the question I asked higher

authority a while ago," Wolfram replied. "An hour out of Ishbaad, to be precise."

"And?"

"And – we close the plant."

"But we don't *know* that this guy's got something going," Kinsey blurted out. "Just because he's a squirrel is no reason to shut him down."

Wolfram frowned at him. "What do we ever *know*, Kinsey? It's what we *think*, right? We jump because we don't have a lot of time to work out legal briefs. We *act.*"

"And we might act wrong." Kinsey stared out at the roiled sea.

"I've said it before. Right and wrong are troublesome words. Technicians should ignore them."

"Even if we suspect this is a heavy ploy by some self-interested institution to cash in some gold bonds?"

"The Bank knows things we don't know, Kinsey. They say cancel some sucker's account, we cancel." He paused. "Is this causing you some problems? Are you with us?"

Kinsey's answer was slow in coming. "Okay, okay. I want to see what happens next."

Wolfram stared at him hard for a moment, then turned back to the others. "Let's go,

102

then. I have to send some messages. Magraw, at three o'clock put into some cove, and we'll work out a plan."

They anchored in shallow water off a small island dotted with bleak ruins. A dozen gulls brooded on the shoreline. Others glided in long arcs overhead.

The group sat in the windowless, cool chart room. Unrolled on a folding table was the map of the Isle of Ishbaad.

Wolfram used the emir's pen as a pointer. "All right, what do we know? Harada, what about security?"

"The oil tanks, the fortress, and the dock are spotlighted." the Japanese said, indicating features on the map. "In addition, each light tower has a closed-circuit television camera. There are guard posts set here, here, and here. There are motorized patrols covering the perimeter of the island by road. I saw no foot patrols along the shoreline. It's very rocky.

"Okay," said Wolfram. "Hamir, what did you pick up?"

"Several warning signs of some interest. The nitration plant area inside the fortress had numerous warnings saying 'Danger, High Explosives. No Smoking. Special equipment must be worn.'"

Hamir indicated a small shed near where their limousine had stopped. "A sign on this building said – and this is most odd – 'Triangle badges must be worn before descending.'"

"Descending?"

"Exactly."

"The shed was an elevator housing, perhaps?" asked Magraw.

"It did not say. My guess is yes. Or a stairwell."

"To the caves, you think?"

"It is possible."

"Triangular badges were called for on some other signs. Identification of some sort."

"Or radiometers," said Wolfram. "If we put that together with what Juanita found?"

"You have some dangerous radiation source," said Magraw. "One that used a water cooling system."

"That might explain the fake oil towers," Harada noted. "Nuclear facilities require fresh water, demineralized."

"What's it mean, Magraw? You're the engineer."

The black man puffed on his cigar. "I'd guess a nuclear reactor. What they call a 'swimming pool' reactor maybe."

"The bastard *is* making an A-bomb!" Kinsey snapped.

Wolfram shrugged. "Maybe. Maybe not. If he is, he can't deliver it with the Styx-type missile he was talking about." He twirled the emir's pen in his fingers. "What about this? Could his reactor have something to do with a pen?"

"How?"

"I can't figure it. But" – he looked up at them – "that can wait. Right now we have to work out the plan to scrub the emir's island." He pointed at the Turkish fortress on the map. "The key is the nitration facility. If it goes, it takes out the oil storage and probably most of the rest of the island."

"But, it's spotlighted, guarded, and monitored on TV," said Harada.

"Correct. But that old, dry cistern is not. And, it abuts the shoreline. A couple of tons of explosives in there would do it."

"A couple of tons!" Kinsey exploded. "Hell, we couldn't get a couple of *pounds* in there before we'd be spotted."

Wolfram nodded. "My plan is to infiltrate explosives into the cistern from the sea." He tapped the map again and indicated the jagged coral islands just south of Ishbaad. "Our base, such as it is, will be here, at the

105

Kettles. We'll have to keep the ship out of sight over the horizon."

"What," said Magraw. "I thought we'd agreed that we couldn't smuggle the explosives into the cistern without being seen."

"Correct," said Harada. "We could put one of the fortress searchlights out of commission for a short time, along with its TV monitor, but it would create suspicion. Even so, there would not be enough time to plant *tons* of explosive. And what about transporting this material to the beach?"

Wolfram held up his hand. "Hold on. You're all talking about moving solid-state explosives in there. In fact, my plan is this.

"First, as Harada suggested, we will neutralize the TV monitor problem –"

"How?" Magraw interrupted.

"With *mirrors*. But I don't want to get into that just yet. Let's get the explosives problem out of the way."

Kinsey snorted. "Right."

Wolfram ignored him. "There is one extremely effective explosive that is *liquid* at the kinds of temperatures we have here."

"*Nitro?*" exclaimed Magraw.

"My plan in essence is to pump our explosives from the corol island through a long pipe leading into the cistern. It's a distance of less than a mile in shallow water. That done, we give it the spark. The detonation unquestionably will touch off the nitration plant nearby. Also, there probably are inventories of the emir's rocket propellant stored there.

"The series of detonations almost surely will touch off the oil storage.

"Finally, and maybe most important, we will count on the exploding cistern to split the rock strata leading into the caves under the island." He held up a sketch he had made of the cistern, and a profile of the island shore. "As you can see, the cistern floor is well below sea level. So are the caves. If we can open some entries, the Red Sea will drown out the interior of the island."

"But the *nitro*," Kinsey protested. "You're talking about handling *tons* of the stuff. Does Magraw drag a bargeful up from Aden? And how do we keep from blowing up every time we cough?"

Wolfram, who had the answers, said nothing.

After the meeting had adjourned, Wolfram grasped Hamir by the elbow. "I have a special mission for you."

"I fear I have little experience or talent for your kind of work, Hugo."

"But you do have experience as a courier, an observer. You do know the language, and you're familiar with Al Hakeer."

"That's true. The Bank has an office there that I sometimes use."

They walked out on deck. Wolfram seemed preoccupied and spoke only after a long silence. "I want you to go to Al Hakeer."

"When?"

"Now."

Hamir glanced toward the coast, a strip of ocher on the horizon. The wind had stopped, leaving behind it a thin veneer of grit over everything. "We are many miles from Al Hakeer."

"Kinsey can fly you back to within a few miles of the city. Can you manage the rest of the distance on foot?"

"I think so. There's a highway along the coast. After sunset the heat will not be so ferocious. What am I to do?"

From his shirt pocket Wolfram withdraw the emir's pen. "You have one of these, too."

"Yes."

"Take both yours and mine." He clipped his into Hamir's pocket. "I want you to get the first flight you can out of Al Hakeer. What might that be?"

"There's an early morning flight to Cairo or an afternoon flight to Aden."

"Is your Egyptian visa still valid?"

"It is."

"Good. Then go there. This is important. Take the pens to the Bank's people there. They'll know what to do, if they get my message without garbling. This is what I want done with the pens."

Hamir took out his notebook, and Wolfram dictated.

"Metallurgical analysis with electron microprobe of all the materials in the pens. Elements, significance of the alloys, if any. Chemical analysis of the ink – it is explosive and, if so, will it trigger the alloys in any way? Is it poisonous? Could this pen conceivably be used as a chemical or nuclear device, a component of same?

"After you have delivered the pens, return immediately to Al Hakeer. Make your base in the Bank's office."

"What do I do there?"

"Can you see the Isle of Ishbaad from it?"

"Easily."

"Observe if the emir leaves the country, how he leaves, and his destination."

"He might leave secretly, or at night."

"I don't think his rhetoric will let him. As

109

Ramadan approaches we'll hear more from you. You'll hear him on Radio Hakeer."

"How do I get word to you?"

"Through the Bank. How do you communicate with them?"

"In clear on commercial telegraph – a word code, of course, but no cipher. They are suspicious even of that." Hamir smiled. "Even straightforward money transactions tend to look like code."

Wolfram thought a moment. "We can't have any delay. Do it this way. Reverse the itinerary. Instead of any reference to Al Hakeer, make it Aden. The message will refer to –"

"Banker's acceptance," suggested Hamir.

"Good. It sounds like a real bank transaction. If the emir leaves Al Hakeer, goes to Cairo, and has a destination on the twentieth in London, your message would be something like 'Banker's acceptance will leave London via correspondent bank in Cairo, arrive Aden on twentieth.' Clear?"

"What if I am questioned on this 'banker's acceptance'?"

"The Bank will cover," Wolfram said.

Hamir hoped so.

Well after dark the glass-eyed helicopter swooped out of the darkness, its rotor whipping the placid sea to a froth before it settled lightly on its home barge.

After they had helped him rebundle the craft inside its protective cocoon of nylon tarpaulins, Wolfram asked the pilot, "How was he?"

"Nervous, but otherwide looking like a proper banker. All three buttons on his jacket were buttoned. His necktie was straight. He carried his briefcase in a correct banker way. He looked just like any other businessman you'd run into wandering along an Arab highway."

"Let's hope the road isn't patrolled. How far from Al Hakeer did you land him?"

"I made it less than five miles."

"He should have no problems."

"Not unless somebody thinks he stole those ball point pens."

They took the launch back to the minesweeper. Above them the Arab sky glittered with stars. There was no moon, and the clear, dry air seemed to bring the constellations closer.

After the others had turned in, Wolfram poured himself a Scotch. Then he strolled to the radio shack, where he put on the earphones and began the laborious task of patching a voice circuit together over a network of secure lines. It took thirty-three minutes.

"Chairman here."

"Wolfram."

"Go ahead."

"Re your earlier message, I have a plan to close the plant."

"Good. Is this a permanent closing, or temporary?"

"Rather permanent."

"Excellent."

"I'll need an airdrop as soon as possible."

"I'll put on a recorder. You dictate your requirements."

"Before you do, there's something you ought to know."

"Oh?"

"I have reason to believe that our client fully intends to carry out his rather large-scale program, the one he has referred to in his communications."

"His reference, as I recall, was to a certain aggregation of – leaders."

"That's it."

"What has to be done?"

"This might involve some kind of radioactive material."

"Yes."

"Radiometers will be required at ports of entry, within certain offices."

"It might not be possible."

"True. But our client won't know we're looking."

"What do you suspect?"

"There's a very strong possibility of a small nuclear device. An A-bomb."

"But how?"

"By smuggling in small quantities of enriched uranium concealed in large numbers of ordinary, everyday products. The stuff is radioactive, but not particularly dangerous, in small, separated amounts. Pull them together into a critical mass and you start a chain reaction – *Wham!*"

"What does this enriched uranium look like? How much is a critical mass?"

"It looks like a blackish metal. Very heavy. A critical mass doesn't take up much room. Check the atomic energy people but I think you can get an explosion out of as little as twenty-six pounds."

"Did you see any of this stuff? Facilities to make it?"

"No," Wolfram conceded. "But there's nuclear activity there. We know that."

"Have shipments been made yet?"

"We don't know. But you'd better get the radiometers working. We can close the plant at this end, but some of the products may be in the hands of the distributors."

There was a pause. "We'll try it. It'll be hard to pull off without our – competitors – noticing."

"We don't know the means of shipment, only the approximate time of arrival."

"I understand." There was another pause. "What shape might we be looking for?"

"Ball point pens."

"Ball point pens?"

"Exactly."

"Anything else?"

"No. Put on your recorder, and I'll dictate what we want airdropped."

A moment later there was a bleeping signal. Wolfram recited carefully the co-ordinates for an airdrop into the middle of the Red Sea. Then he specified his needs – a stainless steel portable floating pump, a four-horsepower engine to drive it, and a comparable air compressor.

Two one-mile lengths of one-inch heavy duty flexible plastic tubing.

One mile of insulated copper cable.

A thousand pounds of flaked dry ice in insulated bags.

Eighty-six hundred pounds of acid in two-hundred-pound tanks, the acid to be mixed precisely 52.7% nitric acid and 47.3% sulfuric acid.

114

One ton of $C_3H_5(OH)_3$, known to chemists as glycerin.

Then he signed off.

9

By morning the dry, abrasive wind from the desert had resumed, powdering the sea with a yellow scum. On the dead island, even the gulls were gone.

"Time to leave, Captain Magraw." Wolfram was standing on the bridge with the black man, looking toward the bow, where Kinsey was ready to weigh anchor. Magraw gave him a hand signal, and the flyer thrust the twin clutches of the anchor winch forward.

Magraw put the ship's diesels into reverse, and the minesweeper plowed slowly backward from its berth.

"Where to?"

Wolfram handed him the written coordinates for the rendezvous. "We have an appointment with an airplane."

"One of ours or one of theirs?"

"A supply drop. If we play our cards right, they may not hit us with the stuff."

"Don't *say* that. Those parachutes look like they're floating down as soft as can be, but they hit like cannonballs."

"That doesn't worry me as much as the stuff going right on down to the bottom of the sea."

"Why not use one of these little islands?"

"Too close to the coast. I want to be away from any shore visibility and in international waters."

"Surely you're not having them dump the nitro on us, are you?"

"Yes and no," Wolfram replied. He glanced at his watch. "Which reminds me, I'm having a little seminar on nitroglycerin within the next few minutes. Stick to the heading. I'll fill you in later."

He went below to the chartroom, where the others were waiting, clustered around the folding table. The map of Ishbaad served as a tablecloth. Wolfram moved to the end of the small cabin where there was a blackboard bolted to the bulkhead.

"As we discussed previously, our problem is to introduce a few tons of nitroglycerin into the cistern. As some of us have noted, nitro is touchy, unpredictable, and deadly."

"But we use it anyway?" asked Juanita.

"In this case we *use* it, but we don't *handle* it, not directly. The question is *how?* The

116

answer is, we manufacture the stuff *inside* the cistern."

Harada said softly, "That's rather complicated, isn't it?"

"Not at all," said Wolfram. He scribbled some data on the blackboard and then turned to face them again.

"Nitroglycerin is one of a family of compounds that chemists call *esters*. In fact, they prefer to call the compound glyceryl trinitrate.

"Now, in making this material in large lots, one adds slowly one part by weight of glycerin to 4.3 parts of a mixed acid. The mixed acid is 52.7 percent nitric acid and the rest sulfuric acid. The nitric acid, of course, reacts with the glycerin to create the explosive."

"And what is the purpose of the sulfuric acid?" asked Harada.

"The nitration process creates water as a byproduct, so it's necessary to mix in a material to absorb the water, such as sulfuric acid. It also serves as a catalyst."

"I see."

"So far it seems simple enough," said Wolfram. "However, this process produces a great deal of heat. Consequently, the mixture has to be cooled to twenty-five

117

degrees centigrade or less. It has to be stirred with compressed air."

"What happens if the temperature rises?" Kinsey asked.

"First there is a lovely red smoke. Then, *poof.*" He paused, then went on. "If that doesn't happen – and we intend that it does not – the reaction goes to completion, and the nitro rises to the top of the acid bath and sits there. At the stage it forms the layer on the acid, it is explosive."

There was an uncomfortable silence.

"Now," said Wolfram, "here's how we're going to do the job. Safely."

Wolfram told them about the airdrop and then described how they would run plastic tubing from the tiny coral island into the cistern on Ishbaad. One tube would transport, first, the acid and then, compressed air. The other tube would carry the glycerin. Paralleling them would be an electric circuit to trigger the charge at the appropriate time.

"Unless," he said, "red fumes develop, and our material saves us the trouble of detonating it."

Hamir presented his passport to a scowling, bearded emigration official at the Al Hakeer airport. Hamir was anxious about the fact that this procedure should have been gone

118

through twenty-four hours earlier, but even Wolfram's plans could not obviate the problem of a lack of seats to Cairo.

The official searched the banker's face and then compared what he saw against the blank-faced photograph in Hamir's document. Despite the obvious likeness, the official was deeply suspicious.

Slowly, he turned the pages.

"You are much traveled, Mr. Hamir."

"I'm a banker." He checked his watch. Ten minutes until his flight's departure. Hamir worked to project a calm he didn't feel.

The emigration man scrutinized each page.

"Ah," he said. "There is an irregularity here, Mr. Hamir."

"Indeed?"

The bearded man pointed to the last stamped page of the passport. "You desire to leave our nation, but there is nothing here to show that you arrived, Mr. Hamir. How do you account for that?"

Hamir's thoughts churned in near panic.

"What do you mean?" he stalled. "Here I *am*. Obviously, I arrived."

The official held the passport up for him to see. "Look. There is no official arrival

119

stamp. There must be an arrival stamp for all travelers, unless –"

Obviously, it would do no good to claim a mistake. The entry officer was probably this same man.

"Oh, *now* I see what you're talking about," he chuckled. "That is easy to explain."

"Explain."

"The evening before last I was aboard a small ship, and it docked at the Isle of Ishbaad –"

"You landed at *Ishbaad?*"

"I most certainly did." Hamir forced indignation.

"Proceed."

"Yes. On Ishbaad my colleagues and I were entertained by the emir himself."

The official frowned.

"We have a fine meal, of course. A great man, the emir. He gave me this." He produced one of the pens. "A generous man, as well."

The emigration officer studied the pen carefully. Hamir looked at his watch again.

"Proceed."

Hamir felt sweat beading his upper lip. "Afterward, the next day, in fact, my bank contacted me aboard the ship. We were cruising on down the coast, you see." He gave the name of his Lebanese bank. "You

120

can check with them, of course. They'll verify that. They asked me to leave for Cairo immediately on bank business." He smiled. "Unfortunately, yesterday's flights were booked solid."

It was possible, thought the emigration man, that this man *had* dined with the emir, in which case he was someone to be reckoned with. If he were lying, that, too, could be found out.

"These facts must be confirmed, naturally." He ventured a smile. "You understand. It is just a formality."

"Of course," Hamir smiled back. "Please call the emir."

The emigration man looked pained. "Perhaps we should not trouble him directly. He is most busy. Was there anyone else?"

"Dr. Gamal dined with us. Do you know Gamal?"

"I have heard the name."

"He is on Ishbaad now, I believe. A quick call to him should resolve this matter, if you please." Hamir tapped his watch.

The official picked up his telephone and ordered the Cairo flight delayed until Mr. Hamir could board. Then he placed a call to Ishbaad.

Hamir looked around the small, congested airport lobby. The walls were papered with

121

brightly colored posters featuring the emir's portrait and menacing quotes from his now-famous speech in the square of Al Hakeer. The Lebanese didn't really see them. His ear was tuned to the quiet telephone conversation behind him. Apparently, the emigration man had reached an aide, rather than the doctor himself.

"I see. The doctor is in his laboratory and cannot be disturbed. Perhaps you can tell me, then, a gentleman named Hamir, there was a dinner."

There was a long pause at the official's end of the line while his receiver quacked in Arabic inaudible to Hamir.

"I see, then – the emir gave him a gift *pen* – thank you."

The emigration man snapped the passport shut and thrust it at Hamir. "Please excuse this delay, sir, but Zionists and their agents oppress us. We must be vigilant for irregularities."

Hamir nodded emphatically, stuffed his passport into the breast pocket of his jacket, and strode briskly across the tarmac toward the jetliner. Moments later the huge craft lumbered away from the gate and boomed off into the flawless blue sky.

Exactly one hour later the telephone jangled at the customs desk.

"Yes?"

"This is Dr. Gamal."

"Yes, sir."

"You have cleared a man named Hamir?"

"Promptly, sir, as soon as –"

"He showed you a pen"

"Yes, sir."

"He should have been detained."

The emigration man felt a sudden burning sensation at the base of his sternum. He said nothing.

"Can the plane be recalled?"

"Alas, sir, it is far outside our jurisdiction and, indeed, by now has landed in Cairo."

"Damn him," snarled Gamal. "I knew those pens were trouble."

Before the agent could say anything, the line went dead.

By late afternoon the minesweeper was circling slowly the imaginary intersection that marked its rendezvous point.

"How long will it be?" asked Magraw.

"Hard to say." Wolfram offered him a fresh cigar and lit one himself. The others were below, reading or napping. "Our people had to gather the materials, load it, and then get it here."

"From where?"

"My guess would be England."

"Is it difficult stuff to come by?"

Wolfram shook his head, scattering ash. "No problem."

"Where *is* the problem, Hugo?"

"Just one place, really. Getting our tubing from the sea into the cistern. If the mortar on those old stones above ground has decayed enough, we can just slide our pipe right through the chinks."

"And if it hasn't?"

"We'll have to go over the top rim."

"And that'll put us on the Big Screen."

"That's where the mirrors come in."

"I thought you were kidding about doing it with mirrors."

"The trick is to blind the TV lens. At night, of course, we couldn't do it. Too obvious. In daylight we don't have much going for us in the way of shadows and concealment."

"That narrows the options," Magraw observed.

"But there is one time of day when the camera is blinded naturally, even if only for a couple of minutes."

"How's that?"

"The camera on the spotlight tower faces west. At sundown, it is looking into sun. Whatever image the camera picks up is

124

terribly distorted between patches of very bright and very dark."

"Can we bank on that?"

"Maybe, but we won't. My plan is to reflect light through a prism and focus it squarely on the camera lens. That way we can blind it for, say, three to five minutes. We won't need more than that."

"Who's going to do what?"

"I'll be along to focus on the camera eye. Kinsey will make the climb up the cistern. Juanita will stay underwater to help with the gear."

"It's risky as hell."

"Sure. But Kinsey says he can do it, and I think he can."

"If you say so."

"Look," said Wolfram. "The only thing that TV camera sees is the east half of the cistern and the top. We'll stay in the water well to the lee of its vision. Besides, there'll be a lot of reflection from the sea, and the shore's rocky with coral heads. More than enough for concealment."

Magraw made a noncommital sound.

Wolfram pointed skyward with his cigar. "Is that our contact?"

Magraw brought the minesweeper sharply about to face eastward, out of the sun. "Probably our boy."

Minutes later a C-5 transport without insignia zoomed above them, banked, then slowly circled in until it was a thousand feet overhead.

In the wake of the plane brightly colored parachutes blossomed suddenly. Thermal updrafts from the sea caught the dropping supplies and, for an instant, held them swinging against the sky. Almost reluctantly, they yielded to gravity.

As quickly as it had appeared, the C-5 circled back up into the perfect sky and disappeared in the distance.

Less than a hundred miles away, Gamal spoke with the emir.

"I've been trying to get to you all day."

"I have been with Allah." The emir's voice conveyed apology. "First, I oversaw some of the final work with the reactor. We now have ample material in a form that will allow for optimum distribution. We are ready, Gamal. After completing the work I went straight to the mosque to offer prayers of thanksgiving and to ask, of course, for further guidance."

"The underground mosque?"

"And why not? Allah's work is done there. The greatest single blow that will ever be struck by the Arab world found its genesis there, with His inspiration."

"And my report on the potentialities in radioactive poisoning."

The emir didn't answer him. After a discreet pause, Gamal spoke again. "After dinner the other night, I – suggested – that it was unwise to discuss either cobalt or the pens in the exhibit. I suggested that our visitors might or might not have been what they seemed."

"Go on."

"Today one of your erstwhile guests, the man Hamir, boarded a plane for Cairo with one of those pens."

"How do you know this?"

"I checked the exhibit. Three pens are missing from it."

"But why is this cause for alarm? Those pens are untreated, harmless. What could they reveal?"

"What is important is not that the pens were stolen but that he flew to Cairo so quickly with one of them. I do not believe they took them as souvenirs."

"You're right. Why was he not detained?"

"Our agent wouldn't dream of disturbing you and I was busy in the caves, so the agent went along with the bluff."

"We must watch this carefully." The emir

smiled quickly. "But what does it matter? Even if all of them were spies, what could they have seen that we did not show them? How could they know – even guess – at our plans? Only you know that, Gamal. And I."

"And only you know how the material will actually be delivered."

"Time is on our side. Even the cleverest enemies need time to act, and they require a specific target to act against. These people have nothing except a few metal objects. What could they learn from a simple pen?"

"That it is made of cobalt."

"Even if they solve that riddle, they will be too late."

10

On the eighth day before Ramadan the tide reached the dead low mark at the Kettles at 2:11 A.M. Wolfram's team moved in to establish its beachhead.

Harada rode the bow of the ship's launch, his eyes moving from a night-vision scope fixed to the prow to a cathode ray tube on a special depth gauge.

Trailing obediently in the wake of the
128

slowly moving launch, but under its own power, was the minesweeper, connected by a hawser. The barge, in turn, trailed far behind the minesweeper.

"All stop," Harada ordered. At the tiller, Kinsey shut down and then waved a red flashlight twice at the black shape behind them. He heard the minesweeper's diesels ebb, and a moment later, the clatter and whine of the achor descending.

Quickly, he dropped the hawser that bound the launch to the mother ship.

"Okay, Harada."

"Bring her ahead, slowly."

Kinsey started the launch engine again and nudged the throttle into forward. The craft, all its lights extinguished, moved tentatively. Seconds later it thudded gently into sand and lurched mildly to portside. Again Kinsey turned off the engine.

The tiny island, a shoal of dead coral, was filled with a kind of mortar of crushed rock and powdery sand. The sulfurous smell of the tidal pool enveloped them – an odor at the same time fetid and clean.

The two men quickly went over the side of the launch and lashed it with ropes to rocks and outcroppings at the high-water mark. Then, Juanita helping from amidships, they began to unload the scuba equipment, diving sled, air tanks, and other gear, stowing them carefully in spaces above the tide line.

Once the diving gear was safely arranged, the two men unsnapped the launch from the anchoring hawsers, pushed it back into the black water, and took it through the predawn darkness, past the ship to the barge.

All of the large containers dropped by parachute had been left loaded and floating, lashed tightly to the stern of the barge. One by one, Harada and Kinsey cut each container loose and then towed it back to shore. Wolfram, meanwhile, had lowered one of the minesweeper's small outboard boats and gone to the beach to help them unload.

The task of towing, unloading, and arranging went on for several hours. The minesweeper had been brought in to within a hundred and fifty feet of the sand at low tide. The water, beginning its return surge, aided in getting the containerized materials ashore.

They worked in silence, the only sounds the plosh of the sea against rocks and the rush of the mild surf around the sand and their ankles. The chugging sounds of engines, the occasional clank of metal against metal or coral didn't bother them too much, for they were on the side of the island away from Ishbaad.

Handling the containers of acid was the most difficult job. For the airdrop, the loaders had bundled the long tanks into threes, strapped together by steel bands. Each bundle, in turn, had been packed with two others in one floating container. At the beach, Wolfram and the others had to manhandle the containers to free the bundles and then cut the strapping and roll each two-hundred-pound tank to a storage place. There were more than fifty of these tanks altogether, counting the glycerin containers.

When they were finished, Wolfram and Harada arranged a camouflage net over the tiers of tanks and anchored it with coral. High tide would cover them during much of the day, but they would be exposed part of the time, and even though the emir's gunboats could not negotiate the reefs very handily, there was always the possibility of air patrols.

An hour before dawn. Wolfram told Harada. "Time for you to go. We've done what we can here."

"I hate to leave you so exposed."

They shook hands. Then Harada took the small boat back to the minesweeper. He left behind the large launch, tied down firmly

131

against the rising tide, its lines blurred by its camouflage netting.

A few minutes later those on the island heard the thrum of the diesels and the grind of the winch hauling up the anchor. Soon the dark silhouette of the minesweeper dissolved into the night.

The sun was still low over the horizon when Hamir stepped from the morning jet from Cairo. For his return to Al Hakeer he carried only an overnight bag and a briefcase stuffed with covering documents from the Bank reflecting actual as well as fictitious transactions between the Arab city and other parts of the world.

In the immigration and customs area, where two agents were checking papers and personal belongings, Hamir recognized one of them immediately as his antagonist from the previous day.

Should he step directly into that man's line, greet him as an old friend, or ignore him, hustle away in the other direction? He opted for the latter. He edged into the other line and adjusted his dark glasses regularly to keep his hand in front of his face as much as possible.

Everything went smoothly. At the end of the process, his inspector handed him his passport and pushed his bag along. "Thank you, Mr. Hamir. Please proceed." Hamir picked up his small bag and strode briskly toward the swinging door marked "Transportation."

Ten seconds later the name "Hamir" registered on the consciousness of the other agent, who had been busy with his own group of passengers. Swiftly, he turned to see only a man's back on the other side of the swinging door. To his colleague, he snapped, "That man you checked through."

"Yes?"

"Registration card, please."

"You know him?"

"Take over here. I must make an important call." He hurried to his office and put through a call to Ishbaad.

"Dr. Gamal! Quickly, please! It is urgent!"

"He is at his office in Al Hakker today."

The agent called the Al Hakeer number.

Finally, "Gamal here."

"Doctor, this is Agent Mahmoud of the Immigration Service. We spoke yesterday."

"Yes, Mahmoud. What is it?"

"The spy, Hamir, has returned."

"Who said he was a spy?"

"You said –"

"That he should have been detained. I

don't know that he is a spy. What have you done with him?"

"We let him go on his way."

"You said nothing to him?"

"Nothing."

"Give me the information on his registration card."

The agent told him that Hamir was staying at Al Hakeer's finest hotel and that his business office was nearby. He read off the telephone numbers of each.

"You have done well. From now on I will handle this matter, and you are to say nothing to anyone about it."

"I understand. But what if he attempts to leave again?"

"Let him go, unless you hear the contrary from me."

In the rainbow groves of coral just west of the Isle of Ishbaad the three of them uncoiled fat spools of plastic tubing and twined it, yard after yard, toward the cistern.

The wound coils, nearly weightless in the sea, were not so difficult to move as to handle in the run of the incoming tide. Wolfram and Kinsey paid out the lengths, while Juanita, using the diving sled, led the twin lines along the shoreline at a depth of fifteen to thirty feet. From time to time she stopped and taped the pairs of tubing together with friction cloth.

By noon, the twin tubes had been extended all but a fraction of the distance to their destination on the western slope of the island. For the third time, Juanita anchored the ends of the tubes to the bottom. Then she took the diving sled back along the route to the Kettles to pick up a fresh air supply. She parked the sled in a triangle of coral and surfaced in the shelter of a large rock near Wolfram and Kinsey.

"How does it go, *machacha?*" asked Kinsey.

"Well."

"Are you tiring too much?"

"A little ache from breathing compressed air so long, but I can finish this. The diving sled makes it easy."

"It must be murder maneuvering this stuff along, dragging a mile of plastic," said Kinsey.

"I'm glad the hoses are buoyant. If it were cable, I couldn't do it."

"I hope our buoyant tubes aren't surfacing."

"I've run them through coral arches."

"Good."

"What now?" she asked.

"Rest awhile. We're well ahead of

schedule." Wolfram smiled. "As long as we have everything and everyone in place before the sun touches the horizon."

The receding tide tugged at Juanita as she moved to a niche in the shadows of a coral formation and shrugged off her tanks. She curled up on the stones and fell asleep with the tepid waters swirling around her.

At almost that same moment, in the Bank's office in Al Hakeer, Hamir received a telephone call.

"Hamir, here."

"Welcome back to Al Hakeer," a voice said in English.

"And who is this?"

"Dr. Gamal."

"Delighted to hear from you again, Gamal."

There was a pause at the other end and then, "Aren't you curious how I knew you were here?"

"No. But, since you bring it up, *how?*"

"Our immigration agents." Gamal chuckled. "They see spies on all sides."

"Their vigilance is commendable."

"Naturally, they consider you a spy."

"Many people see bankers as sinister forces."

136

"Yes," said Gamal. "Be that as it may, it is time for luncheon. You must join me."

"Well –" lunch with the Palestinian doctor could be a mine of significant trivia – "I don't want to intrude on your time."

"Nonsense!"

"Very well, then."

"Excellent. Your office is just around the corner from mine. Why don't you come over now?"

"All right."

"I have a few things to clean up here, so just make yourself at home in the reception area."

"Fine."

"See you shortly."

The line went dead. Hamir stared thoughtfully at the receiver and returned it to its cradle. Knowing these people as he did, he was certain that if they knew or even seriously suspected that he was a spy, he now would be decorating some steaming jail, under interrogation.

Ten minutes later he entered Gamal's office on the eleventh floor of a new office building. The reception room was empty. A desk for an aide or nurse was in one corner, vacant, its occupant probably at lunch.

The room, paneled in cyprus wood, was nearly devoid of furniture, unlike the usual

137

doctor's waiting room. Marks in the carpeting indicated that a number of chairs had been there until recently, but now only one heavy chrome and leather chair and a small octagonal table strewn with magazines remained.

Hamir went to the chair and sat down.

From inside the closed inner office, Hamir could hear Gamal talking loudly on the telephone – some incomprehensible medical dialogue.

Casually, Hamir rummaged through the dogeared magazines, typical medical office fare. A desk set caught his attention. One of the pens looked like the ones taken from the emir. He picked it up and looked at it closely.

No difference.

At that moment he heard his name called from the inner office. "Come in, come in."

Hamir returned the pen to its place, stood, and entered.

"Shut the door, if you will."

Silently, Hamir pushed the metal door into place. "You're looking well, doctor."

"And you, too, Hamir." Gamal's expression was cool, professional. "Any complaints? Fever? Nausea?"

Hamir laughed. "As long as the air-conditioning works, I'll be fine."

"Then your appetite is in tune for

138

luncheon." The physician stood. He wore a business suite. He might have been any Middle Eastern businessman about to close a deal on a shipment of rugs.

"I hope our luncheon won't inconvenience your patients," the banker said.

"Oh, I have none," Gamal replied. "I am strictly a consultant."

"Oh?"

"Let's go." Gamal gestured toward another door. "This way. A short cut."

The minesweeper drifted along in the hot, silent bowl of the Red Sea. On the bridge Magraw was at the helm, puffing his cigar, wondering how things were going elsewhere.

Below, in the radio shack, earphones clamped to his head, Harada listened to the crackle of a designated frequency. The digital clock on the console registered 12:57:33.

At that moment there was a prolonged bleep on the circuit, followed by a coded recognition signal. Harada switched on the recording equipment and transcribed the staccato message that followed.

For the next forty-five minutes, he translated the gibberish of five-figure groups of digits into letters, words, and sentences.

The message was about pens. First, they were made from an unusual alloy consisting

139

primarily of the element colbalt. Second, from an applied scientific standpoint they could be employed only for the writing of messages. Third, they did not write very well.

They lingered over coffee, each reluctant to let the other go while critical questions remained unanswered.

"You see," said Gamal, "The emir has a vision wherein the world once again answers to the Sword of Islam."

"Or to the Arrow of Allah," said Hamir. "But what of you, Gamal? Where does the Arab physician fit in?"

Gamal studied the banker's face. It both troubled and intrigued him that he had shared lunch with a man already dead. The difference between the quick and the dead was, after all, only the microcosmic gap between harmless cobalt and its unstable isotope, cobalt 60.

"I'm a Palestinian, Hamir, a wanderer without his own land to wander in. So I ply my trade, medicine."

"You can deal with the emir at the technical level. You don't have to grope with his metaphysics all of the time."

"Physics, metaphysics, they're all the same to him."

140

Hamir sipped his coffee. "But what's all this about Ramadan?"

"Who knows? It might mean he is taking a vacation."

"Surely, an Arab emir doesn't go to the beach. I mean –"

"Why not? In fact, he leaves today."

"Oh? Where's he going?"

Gamal glanced at his watch. "He leaves in an hour or so for Freeport."

"A nice spot, the Bahamas."

"One of his ships is already there." He tapped his temple with a finger. "A goodwill cruise to celebrate Ramadan."

"Why not? He can afford it."

"Then he is going to fly over to the States. He went to school there, you know."

"New York?"

"To Miami, in fact. An odd destination for an Arab Muslim mystic, wouldn't you say?"

"Ummm."

Gamal glanced at his watch again. "I'm afraid duty calls. I'd better get to the airport to see His Highness off."

"I've enjoyed lunch, Gamal."

"Will you be staying long?"

"Duty calls me, too. Back to Cairo in the morning. Then, who knows?"

The physician grasped his hand. "I'll say goodbye, then. Until we meet again."

11

The setting sun bathed the rocky western edge of Ishbaad in a spectrum of reds. Just offshore, well below the surface, three black shapes waited patiently. With gloved hands they clung to sea fans and handles of coral as the surge and wash of the flooding tide tugged them to and fro. The only sounds came from the ghostly pulse of their breathing equipment and the rush of bubbles flowing upward.

Wolfram moved from his handhold, tapped each of the others on the arm, and pointed at the large dial of his underwater watch. Kinsey, out of his element and ungainly in his diving gear, nodded. Juanita moved downward to the jagged bottom, where they had anchored the coiled ends of tubing, the spare equipment, and the diving sled. She brought up the joined twin ends of the tubing and hooked them into Kinsey's equipment belt.

Slowly, surely, Wolfram and Kinsey

dragged themselves from rock to rock along the bottom toward the shoreline. The twin coils of tubing undulated behind the flyer like enormous prehensile tails leading back to the place where Juanita paid out the hosing evenly. Looped around Kinsey's chest and shoulder like a bandolier was a length of thin nylon line that could more than support his weight. A light, triple-pronged steel grapnel dangled from one end.

At the shoreline, Wolfram again nudged Kinsey and held up five fingers, a reminder that he had no longer than five minutes to make his inspection of the cistern and, if necessary, scale it.

Kinsey nodded, then unhitched his diving tanks and lead belt, and let them sink. For the moment he retained his face mask and mouthpiece. Instead of swim fins he wore black sneakers with boating soles. His face had been stained black to absorb the fading light of sunset. He gave a thumbs-up sign to Wolfram.

Carefully, Wolfram extracted his prism and telescope and bolted them together. Then, removing his mask and mouthpiece, he moved to the surface for a quick look.

The position was correct. The sun was where it ought to be, just touching the horizon, its last light reflected from the lens of the TV camera on its tower. There was no sign of anyone along the treacherous shoreline.

Wolfram ducked back beneath the surface and gave Kinsey the go-ahead. Quickly he resurfaced, his feet braced against a coral head, and sighted his optical equipment on the sun and the camera eye. The dot of refracted light danced on the camera housing. Moving slightly, he beamed it directly into the lens. Surf currents jostled him, and his sighting bounced on and off the camera eye.

At the same time Kinsey crawled out of the water and scuttled the few feet to the base of the cistern.

A quarter of a mile away, in the island's security headquarters, a guard casually scanned the twelve television monitors. According to the room's big clock, it was time to fill in the half-hourly notations on the log indicating what was happening at each monitor site.

Clipboard in hand, he began the check.

Monitor #1 (Viaducts). "A small tanker, *Shigeta Maru,* is casting off."

Monitor #2 (West Storage Tanks). "Nothing."

144

Monitor #3 (East Storage Tanks). "Nothing."

Monitor #4 (Docks). "A large launch has tied up. From it has stepped Dr. Gamal, returned from Al Hakeer."

And so it went, clockwise around the island, to the last image.

Monitor #12 (Fortress area). "Sun and water reflection obscuring the picture at this time of day. Respectfully suggest we change the location of this camera to overcome this problem."

Kinsey saw immediately that there was no chink in the ancient cistern's walls that would admit the tubes.

The rim of the cistern was a good ten feet overhead. By climbing up on a rock he shortened the distance. He unlooped the rope, swung the grapnel in a wide arc, and hurled it to the top.

The first throw bounced back. The second went over the rim, but found no purchase. The third throw held. Twining his legs in the rope, he began to climb, acutely aware of each second's passage.

Clinging, with his feet on the rope and his left arm hooked over the edge of the cistern, he began to unhook the tubing from his belt and feed it over the rim.

The heat was intense, even from the sinking sun, and his black diving suit soaked up every calorie. Sweat ran in a seemingly icy stream from his armpits across his ribs. He took a quick glance at the TV monitor. He hoped to God Wolfram's blinder worked.

Far away he saw a patrol truck rumbling along, headed in his general direction. Had they been alerted? He considered a quick descent and then rejected it. They still had a considerable distance to come.

With his free arm he tugged and hauled the lengths of tubing up and over the side of the cistern. In the water they were weightless. Up here every foot seemed to weigh ten pounds.

Wolfram's instruction was to push the tubing to the bottom of the cistern on the basis that it was only a few feet below the high-tide mark. In fact, it was about ten feet lower and required more hauling and tugging than had been planned. Fortunately, the shadows now were long and stark. Kinsey hoped they camouflaged him.

Finally he felt the vibration of hose hitting bottom. He relinquished his hold on the tubing, lest it start sliding back out of the chamber, and removed a heavy metal staple from his work belt. He pushed it forcefully into a crevice in the stucco and stone, one spike on either side of the tubes. Then, he removed a small mallet and drove the staple firmly into place until it was snug.

Unhooking his left arm from the rim of the cistern, he slid back down the rope. Halfway down the side of the cistern, he drove in another staple to hold the hose. The chink of metal on stone and steel seemed to echo louder than the slosh of the surf on the rocks.

He attempted to jostle the grapnel down, but it was wedged too firmly. Time was up.

Back on all fours again he scrambled back into the sanctuary of the sea, where his companions waited. They used the underwater sled as a kind of tugboat to haul them back to the Kettles. Juanita guided the sled. Kinsey clung to her ankles, Wolfram to his.

Back among the rocks they waded in the hip-deep waters of the tide until each had found a comfortable shelf of stone and dropped tanks and equipment.

"Relax!" Wolfram's shout seemed grating after the silent rhythms of the sea, the whoosh of compressed air, the chink and clank of metal and stone. "We can't get our project going until the tide drops again and we can set up."

"How long?" asked Kinsey.

"Early tomorrow morning. We'll get

147

started around midnight. We ought to be finished before dawn."

They settled in to wait.

Far out at sea Magraw used the sonar to find a shallow ridge, where he dropped anchor. After turning on all of the ship's lights to ward off the remote possibility of a ram by some itinerant oil tanker, he went below to the radio shack, where Harada was monitoring the console. The Japanese poured each of them a Scotch.

"Why do you suppose the emir would use cobalt to make a simple pen?"

That had been troubling Magraw, too. "It's a metal that's used for a lot of things, usually in alloy. They make magnets out of it – tools, instruments."

"And pens."

"Some years back the Big Bomb crowd experimented with cobalt as a casing for nuclear weapons."

"And?"

"On explosion the thermonuclear material turned the cobalt into exceptionally lethal radioactive dust. It was so poisonous it would wipe out every living thing in a major showdown, so they quit using it."

Harada stared at the pen. "What did the cobalt do? How did it get poisonous?"

"Apparently, the explosion turned the cobalt into a deadly isotope."

"Could *that* be radioactive?" He pointed at the pen.

Magraw stood slowly. "If it is, we'd better find out. I'll get the Geiger counter from the barge."

Ten minutes later Magraw came back in and placed the radiometer on the table. "Do you want to turn it on, or shall I?"

"I suggest we pour ourselves a glass of Scotch," said Harada. "The extra time won't make any difference."

They poured, and toasted each other silently.

"Be my guest," said Magraw.

"Honored." With a stage swagger Harada moved toward the little box of technology. Without hesitating, he flipped the switch. The needle on the gauge didn't move.

"Switch it on the fine tune," Magraw said huskily.

Harada turned the dial to pick up faint readings. The needle trembled, but did not swing to the right.

"It means one of three things," Magraw said, rubbing a sleeve across his sweating forehead.

"They are?"

"The damn thing is broken, it's lying, or we're alive."

Harada picked up the pen and waved it in front of the Geiger counter. The needle hopped somewhat, but made no significant movement.

Just then they heard the bleep of the radio signal. "I'll take it," said Magraw. "You pour us some more Scotch." He slipped on the headset and turned on the recorder. During the transmission he scribbled notes and translated key phrases from his own memory of the code.

It took ten minutes.

At the end the black man swung around to Harada, his expression puzzled. "The emir is going to celebrate Ramadan in the States after a stop in the Bahamas."

Harada frowned, shook his head, and drank up what was left in his glass.

12

At midnight Wolfram stirred. In an instant he was awake and alert, eyes scanning the bleak, shadowy features of the tiny island. The air was still and hot, the surf a whisper.

Nearby he saw the shapes of Juanita and Kinsey together on a drift of damp sand. They were eating hungrily from tins of canned meat.

Wolfram sloshed through ankle-deep water to the food container, well above the waterline, as were the other supplies. He selected a tin and wound away the seal as he made a visual inspection of the supplies.

All was in place, much as it had been put down a little less than twenty-four hours before. The camouflage netting dangled strands of kelp and algae.

Putting his food tin down a moment, he hefted one of the dry ice sacks. The outer surface was barely chilled. It was properly insulated, its weight only slightly less than when it was dropped. There would be adequate cooling for their delicate mixing process.

He retrieved his food tin. Like Kinsey and Juanita, he ate with a spoon as he strolled around, surveying their cramped workspace.

"Should we bury the empty tins, Hugo?" Juanita asked him.

"Squash 'em and heave 'em. In a week the Red Sea will have dissolved them." He spooned down the last of his appled pork, crushed the sides of the can, and hurled it out into the darkness.

Through the arch of coral he could see the light towers of Ishbaad, the silhouette of the fortress. The cistern was invisible in shadow from this side. He checked his watch. They were a half-hour into the new day.

"Let's get started."

Inside the island's security, the night guard began the half-hourly check of the monitors. These long hours of the watch drifted in unrelenting tedium. He wished he were back once again with the mobile patrol doing something – anything – to escape the monotony of watching gray images.

Each monitored position revealed nothing except the dull panorama of tanks and docks. Only monitor number eleven showed activity – the mobile patrol grinding along at five miles an hour in its open truck with the machine gun mounted in the middle. The patrol's small searchlight swung this way and that, probing the terrain and the shoreline.

The guard watched as the truck moved outside the range of the camera lens at number eleven and emerged in slightly different perspective in number twelve. The thin shaft of the truck's spotlight jumped along the top of the dimly illuminated fortress wall.

Crawling on past the north corner of the

fortress, the truck paused momentarily as the spotlight brushed over the chain-link gate of the nitration plant. The plant, of course, had its own team of guards inside.

The truck edged on. Now the spotlight danced over the old cistern and flickered at the top of the stone structure. Wait!

The security man leaned forward in his chair and stared at the monitor, even as the truck in the picture moved out of view. Was that the reflection of something at the top of the outer wall of the cistern? The guard peered intently into the grayness, but the closer he leaned to the screen, the more obscure the features of the image seemed.

For a long time he studied monitor number twelve. Nothing moved. He shrugged. Boredom did all kinds of things to the eyes, he thought. When the patrol makes its next round, I'll watch for it again, just in case.

On the log sheet he noted that the patrol had passed posts number eleven and number twelve without incident.

It was nearly 2 A.M. before Wolfram and Kinsey had gotten the pump, compressor, and their respective engines out of their waterproofing and ready to go. One of the plastic hoses was connected to the pump

153

outlet. The intake was served by a large, rigid steel funnel.

The mechanical arrangements finished, the three of them wheeled the heavy acid tanks into place together with the sacks of dry ice chips.

The prospect of beginning the serious work seemed to exhilarate Wolfram. "Now we begin mixing our cocktail. Be sure to wear your gloves at all times. Don't remove your diving suit while we're handling the acid, no matter how hot you get. If any acid splashes on your face, dive in the sea and wash it off. Keep your face masks in place. Okay?"

He pressed the starter on the pump engine. After a few coughs, it thudded into a steady beat that seemed dangerously loud after their long hours of silence. One by one, Wolfram and Kinsey moved the heavy acid tanks into position against the welded funnel and tipped them up. The sour smell of sulfur clawed at their throats.

Meanwhile, Juanita ripped open the heavily insulated sacks of dry ice and dumped the brilliant white flakes into the acrid mixture as it swirled into the impeller and on out through the long tube beneath the sea. After the men emptied each tank, she rolled it down to the surf and, making sure it filled with sea water, submerged it.

They handled the grueling work methodically, with a rhythm that relieved the strain of lifting and handling. When, after an hour, the last gallons of the sulfuric and nitric acid mix disappeared through the pump, Kinsey pushed the empty tank aside and sat down heavily in the sand.

A moment later, Wolfram shut off the pump engine. The silence seemed eerie.

Kinsey gestured weakly. "What about the other tanks, the glycerin?"

"Much lighter. Also, we handle them more slowly. That's the tricky part. But first –"

With one of their wrenches he unfastened the acid tube from the pump and reconnected it to the compressor.

"What does that do?" asked Juanita.

"Out pipeline has a lot of volume, several hundred gallons. The compressor will blow out the acid so it doesn't just sit in the hose, useless."

Wolfram, starting the compressor, timed the operation as carefully as he might clock a race horse. The pressure-gauge needle on the compressor tank crept to the right as the pressure mounted, wavered, then held there. He throttled the engine down. "The compressed air will keep the mixture agitated while we inject the glycerin."

155

Wearily, Kinsey struggled to his feet to help Wolfram connect the second hose to the pump. They began at once the heavy labor of lifting and pouring glycerin into the system for its ultimately deadly bath of acid.

In the security shack the 2:30 A.M. monitor check came and went, but the mobile patrol did not.

The guard again scrutinized the number twelve screen. Nothing had changed. He stood back from the picture. Distance improved the resolution of the image, but it also made the details more microscopic.

Did he see something there? A shape like a – claw?

He squinted. What were those lines on the rim of the old cistern? Did his mind play tricks at this hour of the night? Was there anything there at all?

Movement on monitor number one caught his eye. At last the mobile patrol was resuming its rounds. The truck seemed slow this round. It stopped near the docks. The searchlight bobbed. The driver dismounted. there was a conversation by the front fender.

"You fools!" the security man shouted at the silent screen. "Move *on!*"

As if they had heard the command, the patrol clambered back into their truck and continued. Slowly, the vehicle slid from one picture to the next.

Now we'll see, the security man thought, as the truck disappeared from monitor number eleven. A moment later it appeared by the fortress wall, its searchlight again scanning along the top, past the north corner, and along the cistern.

"Up!" the guard commanded the screen.

The searchlight played across the small cistern, went elsewhere, and then abruptly skimmed back across the top and down again.

There!

There *was* some kind of clawlike thing there. There *were* lines. Had some of the emir's people been working on a project without proper notice to the security section? Or could this be the work of infiltrators?

He called his commandant out of a sound sleep.

At the Kettles Wolfram signaled Kinsey to take a break.

The two of them were bordering on exhaustion now. Having finished with the acid, they had stripped off their diving suits and were working in shorts. Still, sweat poured from them.

"Ten tanks to go." Kinsey kneaded his

biceps with fingers that trembled with fatigue.

"We'll make it. *Then* we rest."

The emir's commandant of security stomped into the television monitor room and glowered ominously at his subordinate.

"Show me!" He was dressed in full uniform, which explained why it had taken the chief nearly forty-five minutes to respond to the call.

"Monitor number twelve, commandant."

The commander stalked over to the screen and leaned close to look. "I see nothing," he snarled. "You called me for *this?*"

"Please move back, sir!"

The commandant stepped away from the monitor. The guard moved in and pointed to the spot where he had seen the suspicious object. "You see, sir? A clawlike object here, a grappling hook perhaps? And lines. Can you see them?"

The commandant's eyes narrowed. "Perhaps. Perhaps not. Has there been anything else? Have these objects moved?"

"No sir."

"Did you notify the patrol to investigate this matter?"

"Only you have the authority to do that, sir."

158

"Ummm."

The commandant stared. If it turned out to be nothing, he would again appear to be a foolish alarmist, just as had happened the other night with the visiting ship. Still –

"I will order the mobile patrol to investigate this more closely on their next round."

"Very well, sir. However, I believe that from their angle on the ground the patrol would have difficulty seeing the object. Actually, their searchlight seems merely to cause the object to reflect."

"So?"

"If I may be so bold as to suggest, sir, the lines – if there are any – appear to be on the sea side of the cistern. Perhaps a patrol on foot could investigate."

The commandant nodded brusquely. "I'll think about that. Stay at your post and report anything unusual there, anything at all."

When the last of the glycerin had been poured into the system, Wolfram moved the tube from the pump to the compressor to replace the air tube.

"From here on it gets a little more touchy."

"Will we make it before daylight?" asked Juanita. Already the eastern sky showed the first light of dawn, though sunrise was still several hours away.

"No problem. The difficulty is in blowing the glycerin out of the line slowly. If we dump too much into the acid at one time we'll get –"

"Red smoke, right?" said Juanita.

"Red smoke until the cork pops."

"But that's what we want, isn't it?"

"Yes. But all of the glycerin in the pipeline must be nitrated. If a third is still in the hose and not in the reaction, we lose that much effective blast."

She nodded.

"Tell you what," he said. "Take the binoculars and a flashlight up on a high rock and watch the rim of the cistern, while Kinsey and I work the compressor. We'll be switching it on and off anyhow, but if you see any red smoke, give me the signal."

Juanita took the binoculars and a flashlight from one of the containers and then climbed up on one of the coral ledges where she could see both the island and the men.

The binoculars brightened the scene as well as magnified it. The top of the cistern was visible. She could even make out the lines of tubing and Kinsey's climbing rope. The sea wall of the cistern was in shadow at its base, but she could see the pale froth of the surf. But what was that?

What seemed to be small lights were wavering slowly along the shore rocks to the south of the fortress.

"I think there is a patrol on the shore, by the fortress!" she called down.

Quickly Wolfram clambered up to where she was perched and took the binoculars. "You're right. We have only a few minutes before they reach the cistern and maybe only a few more after that before they chop the lines." He handed the glasses back to her. "We'll take it slow until they get right up to the cistern. When they do, you give the shout. We'll go all out with the compressor and hope to hell we have enough juice inside the island to open her up."

A moment later the compressor thudded into action, the sound clattering from the hard coral surfaces of the Kettles, out across the water.

The commandant heard the sound as a far-off buzz, like that of a distant motorboat. Who could be operating at this hour of the day? He found secure footing on a rock and turned his glasses in the direction of the sound. It came from the Kettles, an odd and treacherous place to run a boat. He could see nothing.

161

"What is it, commandant?" asked the patrol sergeant.

"An engine, of course."

"A spy's boat, perhaps?"

"Don't ask foolish questions. Tell the men to be very alert."

A moment later the sound stopped. The entire patrol halted and listened for further signs. They scanned the sea for small craft. After a few minutes, the commandant ordered his men to proceed.

The rocks were steep, slippery, and sharp where the sea had fragmented the coral, and the wall of the fortress left them only a narrow access route. In another hour the incoming tide would further restrict their movements.

Their garrison boots were hopelessly inadequate for scrambling on rocks. They needed rubber cleats, not leather, for this kind of work. The commandant swore as his foot skidded from one rock face and his ankle rapped sharply against another. Arms flailing, he skinned his knuckles attempting a handhold. His submachine gun swung awkwardly and clanked against stone.

They inched their way along the western face of the old fort. As they went they scanned the wall, the rocks, and the water. From time to time they would again hear the far-off sounds of an engine. Each time they stopped to scan the sea. The sounds echoed off the hard surfaces around them and then died away.

A quarter of an hour later, the patrol finally reached the side of the cistern that fronted on the sea.

"Look, commandant!" the sergeant exclaimed excitedly. His flashlight played along a rope and some hoses leading into the water.

"Sergeant, climb that rope and cast your light inside."

The sergeant scrambled to the rope and began to struggle up. The other members of the patrol focused their lights around him. One beam strayed higher, to the top of the cistern.

"Commandant!" a voice shouted. "There is smoke rising! Red smoke!"

At that instant Juanita relayed the same message to Wolfram.

"Come down!" he ordered, switching the compressor on again. "Take cover."

Wolfram moved to a shielded spot where he could watch the activity on Ishbaad with the binoculars. He could see the shapes of soldiers clustered at the base of the cistern and strung out along the west wall of the fort, their flashlights flickering. One man was trying to scale Kinsey's rope.

The smoke was clearly visible now, curling heavily at the rim, reluctant to rise into the cooler air.

Wolfram began counting. Any second now.

A brilliant flash punched a huge white hole in the darkness.

Wolfram ducked instinctively, his arms clutched over his head.

Seconds later there was a numbing *wham*, and shock waves like giant hands clapped his ears. Almost instantly the first blast was followed by a second, the sound seemingly muffled. Then came a series of small, hard thumps, followed a full second later by an enormous, pressing *whumpf*.

Oil tanks.

Darkness was washed away now in a great orange light that illiminated the Kettles like a beacon. Above the Isle of Ishbaad hung a flaming ball of rolling yellows, reds, and blacks, fed in staccato bursts of oil from the tanks below.

Where the fortress had been there now was only an obscene bank of white smoke, bloating slowly in all directions. The sea was whitened by a rain of stone, metal, and timber in a vast circle. Pressure waves pushed angry windrows of sea toward the Kettles. They hit with resounding smacks that sprayed droplets and foam over everything.

A vortex a hundred yards wide was forming under the bank of white smoke. The movement was slow at first, but then became faster and faster as it turned into a whirlpool sucking floating splinters and jetsam into its maw.

PART THREE
The Great Rooms

13

It was 8 A.M., the seventh day before Ramadan.

Except for the icons of Arab nationalism nailed to the oak paneled walls, this was a stereotypical boardroom, thickly carpeted, heavily draped. The Moroccan leather chairs and the banquet-sized center table suggested the presence somewhere nearby of large volumes of currency. In fact, until recently these premises had been the command center of one of Tripoli's larger European-dominated financial syndicates.

Now a stark quotation of the Prophet hung in the niche where the picture of a managing director had once been, and before it, the image of Il Duce.

For this occasion the financiers had returned with official blessing.

"Therefore," their spokesman, a round, pink Swiss, was saying, "we find ourselves unable to underwrite your proposal at this time."

Emir al-Mazir al-Hakesch al-Saloud listened to the verdict stoically.

His minister of finance protested. "How can this be, gentlemen! Surely, our gold, our oil reserves, count for something."

"My dear minister," the financier replied, "we have taken that into account. But we must confront the facts. Your gold, all of it, is in escrow, committed to backing your bonds. Your available oil supply is totally committed to servicing that debt."

"But our reserves! Our oil in the ground."

The Swiss gentleman sighed. "With the international money markets what they are at this time, we find ourselves unable to make a commitment against reserves that have not been seriously tapped – as is the case here."

"Your decision is final?" The emir spoke softly.

"At this time it must be, emir."

The emir stood slowly and looked around at each of them. "Then, I must accept your decision, *at this time.* I leave Tripoli within the hour. Perhaps the next time we meet all things will have changed."

He bowed to them, turned, and left, the minister of finance at his heels. "Do not be concerned, emir," he said. "They will come to their senses. The world need for oil will loosen their purses."

"The world will be a different place for
170

them before they know it, perhaps by the end of Ramadan."

In the office complex outside the boardroom the emir's guards and aides waited. One of them, a naval officer, approached him.

"Sir, we have received a request from our Tripoli consul that you contact him at once."

"What does he want?"

"It is a message for your ears only. Most urgent."

"Get him for me."

They moved to a nearby office. The aide put the call through and handed the receiver to the emir.

"What is it?" he demanded.

The emir's expression dissolved into shock. He listened, nodding. Occasionally he interjected a curt question.

"So be it," he said finally. "Send this message to them. 'Your emir, by the will of Allah, continues with his mission. His heart and prayers are with his people.'"

Slowly, he replaced the telephone in its cradle. Turning to the others, he said, "There has been a disaster. The nitration plant on the Isle of Ishbaad has exploded. The Isle of Ishbaad is destroyed." He drew himself up. "It is a sign from Allah himself, a vision of the world of the infidels. This is the will of Allah. We go on!"

Leaving the greasy smear of disaster behind, the minesweeper plowed south at top speed, its destination Djibouti on the African coast.

A platoon of dolphins leaped and dived around the bow of the ship.

"Seems almost peaceful, doesn't it?" said Magraw. "There's always this feeling of relief when we've finally put one of Wolfram's genies back in the bottle."

Harada smiled and then checked his watch. "It's past noon. I'd better wake him and hand him his new stack of problems." The decoded messages, filed in chronological order, still seemed cryptic, ominous. He picked up the clipboard with the tests and then left the coolness of the bridge for the clutching heat outside. The physical impact of the noon sun was a harsh reminder of the predawn. It was just a matter of hours ago, but it seemed a month.

He tapped on Wolfram's door and entered, turning on the light. Gingerly, Harada touched Wolfram's shoulder. The eyes were open instantly, the brain behind them engaged.

"Relax," Harada said hastily. He pulled up a chair.

172

"What's the time?"

"A little after noon."

"I could use another six hours."

"Okay. You want to see these messages first?"

He sat up on the edge of his bunk and took the clipboard from Harada. Meticulously he began reading the messages word for word. His brow furrowed in concentration as he read several messages over twice or three times.

When he finished, he handed the clipboard back to Harada. "Time," he murmured. "We're running out of time. How many hours are we out of Djibouti?"

"About twenty."

"Good. Send this message in the J-4 code."

Harada transcribed.

"'One. Buy bonds. Two. Need translantic jet this time tomorrow to fly Bahamas. Rendezvous Djibouti. Three. Have Atomic Energy Commission authority on radioactive materials stand by for consultation, via scrambler, at 5 P.M., Red Sea Time. Also the Chairman. Four. Instruct Hamir to proceed to Washington, D.C., report to Bank, await instructions.'"

Harada looked at him. "Something is in

173

the wind. The mission isn't finished after all."

"Call me for the scrambler hookup at 4:45. We'll get the others up later. Eat about 6. Then we'll have a meeting."

Harada stood, smiling ruefully. "And here we thought that painted sky was the end of it."

The emir's plane pursued time westward. After refueling in the Azores it embarked on the last leg of its course into Freeport. Even the least among the entourage knew that the destruction of Ishbaad's oil stores effectively forfeited the tiny emirate's treasury and jeopardized its future.

Continuing messages from Al Hakeer brought confirming details of the extent of the holocaust and its repercussions. These communiqués were carried from the plane's message center to the emir by the finance minister.

"There still is no word of Gamal?"

"It is known only that he returned to the island yesterday. It is presumed he went to his projects below the surface. As you know, the sea has flooded into that area."

"These events are in the hands of Allah. His meaning is His own. It is for us only to discern His meaning."

"Of course."

"How long will it be before we can again ship oil?"

"Many months, emir, perhaps more than a year. And the restoration will require funds. We may have to invite in the foreign oil interests again, and their terms will be harsh."

"Could this have been sabotage?"

"But how? The island was well guarded. There were electronic surveillance systems. Not a hint of intrusion. Except for the foreigners –"

"And one of them was an authority in explosives."

"How could he, or anyone, have gotten into the nitration system? It had its own high fence, and around that fence were the walls of the fortress itself."

"True," the emir agreed absently, but, he wondered, how would *he* do it? An electronically guided bomb? No. One had to consider the more likely probability of the nitration process – dangerous at best – triggering itself, despite their precautions.

"Is everything in order in Miami? Arrangements checked and double-checked?"

The minister restrained a sigh. This was the fourth time in as many hours that the emir had asked. "Everything is confirmed, sir – the rooms, the truck, the equipment, the motorboat. All bought and paid for under cover names. Everything as you directed."

"Good, good. The gold doesn't really matter after all, does it?"

"This has been most revealing, most important," Wolfram said to the atomic energy technician at the other end of the scrambler telephone system. "Please put the Chairman on now."

An instant later there was a greeting that sounded like static.

"What do the reports from Al Hakeer look like? asked Wolfram.

"The plant is closed. Our portfolio has been enhanced substantially."

"It won't count for much if the emir works his magic."

"What's that supposed to mean?"

"I mean that even if the emir's plant is closed, *he's* still open for business, and moving."

"We have monitors out. What can he do?"

"He can hit the White House, for one thing."

"Impossible."

"A maximum security effort must be set up."

"You're hallucinating, Wolfram. Get some

sleep. What can one madman do without the bomb?"

Wolfram told him.

At the end of it even the Chairman was at a loss for words.

14

A light wind from the African coast swept across the minesweeper as it approached the western bulge of the Gulf of Aden, closer to Djibouti.

Below decks the air-conditioning hummed, but the chart room was close and humid nevertheless. Wolfram stood before the blackboard. The others, including Magraw, were at their places, dinner dishes pushed aside, coffee at hand. The ship followed the guidance of its automatic controls.

"This, according to his Arab eminence, is mightier than the sword." Wolfram held up one of the emir's pens. "An ancient cliché, of course. We took the words in their more or less original meaning. Our mistake." He paused, looked around at them. "The emir, however, is a literal man in all respects – a

177

technician at one end of the spectrum, a religious fundamentalist at the other. This" – he held the pen like a hypodermic – "is a weapon."

"But the pens are harmless, Hugo," Harada observed. "Magraw and I checked them out with the Geiger counter."

"This is harmless now. But, of course, it can be made lethal –"

"By a nuclear explosion of some kind," Magraw interjected.

"Or by putting it in a nuclear reactor."

Magraw and Harada looked at each other. "We thought there had to be an atomic or thermonuclear explosion."

"Not at all," said Wolfram. "A nuclear reactor creates, after all, merely a controlled nuclear 'explosion.' Nuclear bombardment of ordinary cobalt converts it into the isotope cobalt 60."

"What does this mean?" asked Juanita.

"An instrument, such as a pen, can be manufactured in the harmless cobalt state and then converted into one of the most deadly poisoning agents known to man. A poison that is insidious, delayed-action. It kills many hours, days, even weeks after the victim is exposed. A fatal dose from something like this pen could be as little as three seconds. Theoretically, there is enough potential radioactivity in this pen to kill everyone on the planet. It could kill thousands by simply being put in a congested place – an airline terminal, for instance."

"The perfect assassin's tool," said Kinsey. "You hand it to someone and –"

"But is it the perfect assassin's tool?" asked Harada. "How does the killer insulate himself from fatal exposure while he's doing his deed?"

Wolfram shrugged. "I can only speculate. First, the assassin does not have to be present to do his job. He only needs access to a place his target frequents, or some specific location that he knows the target will go to. He delivers the pen there. In that scenario he could develop a method for shielding himself from the radiation."

"How?"

"A lead-lined suit of some kind, shielded carrying cases, gloves, tongs – a kind of armor."

"A little obvious, isn't it?"

"It would take some clever planning, but it's not impossible."

"What about the other option?" asked Harada. "We are dealing, after all, with a fanatic."

"Very likely. I question that rationale only because such extreme exposure would destroy him very quickly and preclude his covering the target area effectively."

"Who is his target, Hugo? Surely he could get to a small group before he died himself if this cobalt stuff works as you say."

"That's the horrible aspect of this. Remember when we first speculated on what the emir was up to? Our first thought was some kind of warhead, an atomic bomb. What about a hundred, a thousand pens, each placed within reach in every one of the places the president and vice-president frequent?"

"That's fantastic!" Kinsey exclaimed.

"But very, *very* possible," said Wolfram. "What does a pen say to each of us?"

"It says 'pick me up,'" Harada said softly.

"Exactly!"

They all stared at the pen lying on the table. A roll of the ship caused it to move slightly, and they all recoiled.

"Have you warned our people, Hugo?" asked Kinsey.

"All ports, airline terminals, and other entry points are being monitored by radiometers."

"Is it enough?"

"No. It won't stop him because we – our government – is not about to affront a foreign dignitary on pure speculation. Besides, he wouldn't carry the pens with him."

"They can block the radioactive material," said Kinsey, "unless the emir had worked out a plan to smuggle the stuff in."

"I believe he has another plan entirely," said Wolfram.

"Like what?"

"Like a Styx missile."

"You mean *shoot* the pens into – wherever?" asked Kinsey.

"Why not? We know the emir has the missiles and the technical capability."

"Can a Styx carry a payload?"

"This kind, yes," Wolfram replied. "The Styx – officially the SSN-2A – is 6.25 meters long, weighs up to three tons. It is capable of carrying not only a warhead, but a sophisticated and heavy radome guidance system. Take away the weight of the warhead and replace the guidance system with a much lighter, smaller electronic homing beacon, and you have plenty of space to carry, say, a dozen pens and their lead shielding."

"But that means he would have to have an electronic system on shore to home the missile on, which means an accomplice. And what about U.S. radar?"

"Radar is no problem," said Wolfram. "The SSN-2A flies only at fifty meters

181

altitude, well under the radar scan. And it has a range of twenty miles, so the launch could be outside territorial waters."

"But launch from where to where?" Kinsey wanted to know.

"Remember the gunboat that left days ago?"

"Right," said Magraw. "It's a Komar class missile boat. Carries two Styx launchers."

"Okay, okay," Kinsey said. "So tell Washington to intercept the Komar."

"We're a long way from the old Cuban missile crisis. We're past the time when we could scratch an overt menace without a Supreme Court decision on the beauty of it all. Besides, it would become public and that would entail a lot of official explanations."

"So what do we do, Hugo?" asked Juanita.

"We'll try to do something – if you and Kinsey can get to the Bahamas in time."

The late afternoon sun bathed the Komar in a hard amber light.

"It has a fine look, this ship," the emir said to the finance minister as their launch cut across the pale green water of the Freeport harbor. "One day this ship will have a place in the lore of the Arab along with that of the Prophet's horse."

The minister knew better than to question

the emir's Islamic allusions. The man saw symbols in everything. He glanced toward the middle of the launch, where eight compact but extremely heavy metal chests were arranged, each double-locked and sealed. Only the emir had the keys, and only he knew what they contained.

"How long will we remain with the vessel, emir?"

"I shall be here most of the night," he said. "There is much to be done."

The emir caught the question in his subordinate's eyes. "Not work for you, my friend. Your part of the mission will come later, in a few days."

"I am at your command, emir."

"And I trust you."

"I am honored," the minister said.

"When I return tomorrow, we will leave for Miami. Then I will explain your assignment to you."

"Please forgive my curiosity, emir. It is the affliction of one schooled in balance sheets."

"There is nothing to forgive," the emir said. "I would be alarmed if you were *not* curious."

Further conversation halted as the launch swung into position at the Komar's ladder. On deck the full ship's complement had turned out in gleaming whites for the emir's arrival. Once aboard, he turned his attention to the handling of the heavy sealed chests.

Behind him toward the stern of the ship the great twin tubes of the missile launchers yawned emptily. All four projectiles were stowed in specially built heavy steel racks between the launchers, the nose cones positioned for ready maintenance access.

Within the hour an opaque canvas screen was installed around the work area and a large workbench was set up. Sophisticated tools, including an oscilloscope and other electronic test devices, were laid out. Beside the workbench the heavy chests were lined up. Sets of brilliant work lamps were arranged in tiers and switched on, for twilight was deepening.

The emir, in ordinary seaman's coveralls, thanked the captain and his crew for their help. "Now, if you will leave me alone here, I shall pursue my work."

The emir's work continued until nearly 3 A.M. the following morning.

At dawn the Mach Two fighter-bomber landed Hamir at Andrews Air Force Base near Washington. A delegation of men in plain suits from both the Bank and its parent agency, the Company, met him.

"How was the flight?"

"I'm not used to such speed," said Hamir. "It is disorienting. In fact, I feel a bit nauseous."

"It'll pass now that you're back on the ground."

They took him in a limousine directly to a specially secured area on the base where he was ushered into a dimly lit room with one desk and two chairs. In one of the chairs behind the desk sat the Chairman. He studied Hamir as the Lebanese entered and sat down in the vacant chair.

"You look exhausted."

"A trifle ill," Hamir replied. "It will pass."

The Chairman got right to business. "You were in Al Hakeer when we closed their plant."

"The blast cracked the windows of our office. We'll have a substantial replacement cost."

"It was a very effective job, Hamir. Very."

"Thank you."

"Unfortunately, it's not over."

"Oh?"

"There have been peripheral developments. Our plant closing was supposed to abort the emir's plan. Unfortunately, by missing him we still have a problem."

"*He* was never the target."

"Correct," the Chairman agreed. "But

now we know that he should have been part of the target along with his island."

"He is going to Miami via the Bahamas," said Hamir. "I reported that."

"And a significant report it was," said the Chairman, and proceeded to brief the younger banker on the emir's cobalt pens. As he did a ghastly realization began to form in Hamir's mind.

"So you see," the Chairman concluded, "only three of our people have seen the emir close up – Wolfram, Harada, and you."

Hamir, only half-hearing, nodded weakly. Slowly, he took a handkerchief from his pocket and tapped his brow, his upper lip.

"Are you all right?"

"Never again, Chairman."

"What do you mean?"

"I have been exposed to one of the poisoned pens."

"The pens you people took were un-treated, harmless. Wolfram and his people checked them out."

"Those pens," said Hamir. He then explained to the Chairman the details of his previously reported luncheon with Gamal, the doctor's waiting room, and the pen on the magazine table.

"How do you know the pen was irradiated?"

"Please, Chairman. Under the circumstances –"

The old man said nothing.

Hamir looked at his hands, top and bottom. They were the same. "But you see, Chairman," he said with a tight smile, "I am dead."

15

An hour before their jet landed in the Bahamas, Harada awakened Juanita, Kinsey, and Wolfram.

They had slept much of the way, but the Red Sea was far behind. The minesweeper had come perilously close to melting its main diesel bearings on that last leg of the voyage across the Gulf of Aden, for Magraw had pushed the aging vessel hard. Pursuit of the emir had begun.

As a consequence, they had arrived off the port of Djibouti some three hours earlier than estimated. The early arrival gave them extra time to select and prepare the equipment that would be needed in the Bahamas. The list centered on the scuba gear and the diving sled, on which a new power pack had been installed.

Wolfram had made tidy packages of C4 explosives in transparent plastic bags, like small, neat loaves of bread. Then he had picked out detonators.

"Two of each," he had grinned at Juanita as he held up a pair of the gleaming copper tubes. "Remember that – two of each per package of *plastique*."

Their jet aircraft, a DC-10 bearing a triangular insignia and the name "Zambesi Cargo Charter," had rendezvoused, too, ahead of schedule. If the authorities of the Djibouti airport were skeptical of the craft's true identity, they didn't express their doubts. Much of their port's revenue derived from these in-and-out visits by obscure carriers with specious papers.

Wolfram accepted a cup of black coffee from Harada. "What's the status report?"

"The emir's jet left Freeport about an hour ago for Miami."

"Was he aboard?"

"The Company had a man there, but all he could report was that a whole platoon of emirlike people boarded."

"I know what he means. My guess is that he left with them. That means he's in Miami by now. What about the Komar?"

"Still in port."

"Let's hope it stays. At least another twenty-four hours."

"We need to pin down the location of the emir, Hugo."

"Exactly." Wolfram sipped coffee and then rubbed his stubbled chin. "That's why you'll stay in Miami. Try to get close to him at his hotel." He smiled at the Japanese. "Your actor's eye will be able to pick the real emir out from the other."

"Where will you be?"

"We drop Juanita and Kinsey in Freeport with their gear. Then we leave immediately for Miami to drop you. I go on up to Washington."

"Then you see no way of intercepting the Arrow in flight?"

Wolfram shook his head. "There are dozens of routes north. He could be driving, have a chartered plan, train, bus, even boat."

"Those routes are being watched."

"But what are they watching for? The FBI already has a screen watching his hotel, but they don't really know what he looks like. A beard and a Turkish towel.

"The navy is going to try to keep track of the Komar," Wolfram continued, "but if it sails at night –"

Emir al-Mazir al-Hakesch al-Saloud turned slowly from the gold-flecked mirrored wall and stroked his beard pensively.

"The time now has come to change all things," he said.

"Is everything satisfactory, emir?" his finance minister asked anxiously. "The hotel has reserved another entire wing for us."

"Everything if fine. Excellent." The emir glanced out the suite's huge window overlooking the sea. The suite, on the topmost floor of the Miami Beach Hotel, was high enough for him to see the blue line of the Gulf Stream slicing across the pale green of the coastal waters. The sea was calm.

"Come here," he said to the finance minister, who stood and walked over to the mirrored wall.

The emir grasped him firmly by the shoulders and faced him toward the ornately patterned glass. "What do you see?"

"Glass, reflections."

"No, no," the emir said impatiently. "Us! You see the two of us!"

"Of course, Emir."

"And what do you notice?"

"Uhhh – beards? Uniforms? Headdress?"

The emir shook him. "*Look*, man!"

The minister cleared his throat. "Well,

190

there is a resemblance, superficial, to be sure," he added hastily.

"*Not* superficial, my friend." The emir smiled. "The resemblance is very close."

"If you believe so, Emir, I am honored indeed."

"I do believe so, and so do others." He clapped the minister on the back. "That is why you have been selected for an important assignment."

"I have?"

"Yes." The emir looked around. "Do you have the official portfolio? The one with the itinerary?"

"Over here, Emir." The minister handed it to his chief.

"Umm," murmured the emir, studying it. "The visits to the bird sanctury and the aquarium shall be made, but these dinners with businessmen must be canceled. The meeting with the U.S. government representative must be postponed until the end of the week."

"Very well, Emir. Are the scheduled times satisfactory?"

"Are they satisfactory to you?"

"To *me?* Why?"

The emir laughed. "Because you are going to be the watcher of birds and fish. Shoulders back, man! Look like a prince!"

It was past noon when Harada plunged from the hot and humid outdoors into the chilled lobby of the emir's hotel. Removing his dark glasses, he went directly to the information desk.

"The suite of Emir al-Mazir, please."

"Is he expecting you?"

"I am a friend."

"I'll connect you with his appointments secretary."

"Thank you."

There was a brief conversation on the telephone behind the desk. Then a receiver was handed to him.

"Yes?" asked the secretary.

Harada identified himself. "The emir was kind enough to entertain me just a week or so ago on Ishbaad. By the purest chance I learned that he would be in Miami Beach just as I am here on business myself."

"I will make inquiries, sir."

While he waited, Harada scanned the lobby. A handful of guests. None seemed to be interested in him. At the far end of the elevator ranks, the service elevator door opened and a crew-cut waiter in a bright red hotel jacket emerged. He wore large dark glasses. He glanced once in Harada's direction and then scurried the other way on some mission.

Odd, thought Harada – a waiter in dark glasses.

The secretary came back on the line. "The emir is napping now. He has had a long journey and a busy day tomorrow."

"Of course."

"Perhaps, if you call in the morning before nine. After that he plans to leave to see the bird sanctuary."

"Very well. Will you leave my name for him?" Harada spelled it out and then handed the telephone back to the clerk. "I notice even your waiters wear dark glasses."

"Not on duty, they don't, not in uniform."

"I just saw one."

"We will remind the staff."

An odd place, this, Harada thought. Very odd.

The waiter had seen Harada. What, he wondered, was that man doing in this place at this time? An unlikely coincidence.

Quickly, he stepped into a service passage and glanced around. Empty. Good.

The waiter stripped off his red jacket and leather bow tie, rolled them into a ball and threw them into a laundry chute. He then went down steps to the basement and walked purposefully beneath pipes. It was stifling hot here after the chill of the upper floors, but the heat didn't bother him. He brushed his hand along his smooth-shaven chin.

Before long he found a ramp leading to a side street, where he hailed a cab. The Cuban driver mistook him for a countryman and addressed him in Spanish.

"Sorry, pal, I don't speak the language."

"My mistake. You look Latino."

"Jewish," the waiter laughed. He gave the driver directions to an address in Miami proper.

"You from the city?" the driver asked as they motored over the causeway to the mainland.

"Just visiting."

They made small talk about the weather as the cab made its way through the midday Miami traffic.

The address turned out to be a large parking building near midcity. The passenger paid the driver and included a handsome tip.

At the garage office the waiter handed a ticket to the attendant.

"Is that a panel truck? Green?"

"Right."

The attendant brought it around. The waiter took a special key from his pocket and unlocked the back doors. Inside were four heavy metal boxes, which he opened. Each box was lined with what appeared to be a honeycomb of metal, each cavity empty, as he had expected. In a larger trunk was the very special outsized box camera and lens. Another trunk contained accessories, another diving gear.

The waiter locked the doors again, then climbed behind the wheel, started the engine, and drove away slowly. He made his way to the Florida Turnpike and drove north, keeping well within the speed limit. He had a valid license and papers for the truck, of course, but one must play it safe.

At the Fort Lauderdale exit he turned off and followed the road east through the flat neon-cluttered approaches to the coast until he reached a small motel near Port Everglades. A room has been reserved for him there.

Inside his room he sat down for a moment on its one seedy armchair, then picked up the telephone, and dailed a number.

"Harvey's Boat Service."

"Hi. This is Al Mazer. I'm just double-checking on my boat for tomorrow."

"Let me check it." There was a pause, then, "You're all set. Twenty-eight-footer."

"Good. You have the extra anchor? Plenty of line?"

"Check."

"I'm going out early. Will there be someone there to help me with my gear?"

"From 3 A.M. on. Fishermen like to get out early."

"Great."

"You doing a little fishing? We can fix you up with bait, whatever."

"No thanks. Actually. I'll be diving. Underwater photography."

"It'll be dark."

"I want to see the scene when the sun comes up. It's going to be a great day."

16

The Komar seemed tail-heavy. From midships forward the vessel had the menacing shark lines of the classic combat ship. The sole projection was a small but formidable turret with twin twenty-five-millimeter anti-aircraft guns.

But from midship aft, the vessel seemed bloated with a high-rise clutter of bridge-work, masting, and missile launchers. The latter were enormous, each some thirty-five feet long and perhaps four feet in diameter at their widest dimension. They ran along the main deck, rising upward from the stern at an angle of twelve degrees. Basically, they were nothing more than hollow conduits for the missiles, which did all the work of launch and guidance themselves.

This off-center mass of superstructure gave the illusion of pushing the stern low in the waters, for the aft deck was only five feet above the surface. It was difficult to believe that this ungainly seeming craft had the firepower capability of sinking a large battle cruiser under appropriate circumstances.

"The stern is the place we'll go aboard," Kinsey said to Juanita.

The pressure of time had forced them to improvise a plan that was patchier than prudence would dictate, but, there was no choice, for the vessel might depart at any time.

It was dusk now. Kinsey observed the Komar from a lower porthole of a large motorboat retained by the Bank for their mission. They had boarded it earlier in the afternoon at a marina elsewhere on the island. One of the Bank's men had sent their equipment – and them – below decks while he and two others took the large craft out into

Providence channel and maneuvered it during the late afternoon to a pier berth in the Freeport ship harbor.

The Bank's men had made a noisy show of tying the boat up and departing. Their cover story, should anyone inquire, was that the boat was going to go into dry dock for some hull work. To the casual observer the craft now was locked up, dark, and empty at its mooring, some three hundred yards from the warship.

"Time to suit up, *muchacha.*"

They didn't talk as they helped each other into the tight, hot suits and the heavy equipment.

Kinsey handed Juanita her mask. "I blackened the ring with a match to take the shine off." He motioned her over to the porthole. "There are lights all around the harbor, even though our people knocked out the circuit for this pier. The Arabs have the Komar's gangway and foredeck lit up like a carnival."

"Clever," she said. "That way no one looks at their weapons."

"That's a break for us," he said. In the thickening gloom of the cabin he located their night-vision scope and then studied the length of the Komar.

"Look," he said, handing her the scope.

"Two sentries by the gangway, but between the launchers near the stern there's another. See him?"

"How will we chase that one away from the stern so we can do our work?"

"I could make some noise on the other side of the ship."

"Too risky."

After a moment he said. "There's always the knife. Give him a quick one. Drop him in the harbor."

"I couldn't do that."

"I'm not sure *I* could, either." He let his breath out slowly. "I've got it – I think. When they get ready to sail, they'll have to take up their gangway. That's when they'd probably call in their deck watch to stand by their departure stations, right?"

"It wouldn't give us much time."

"It shouldn't take much." He tried to sound confident. "Hell, it'll take them – what? – five minutes to get the anchor up."

"That means only one should go topside," she said. "Me. You stay below for the getaway."

"I'll go up."

"Nonsense. I know exactly what to do to the missiles. You don't."

It was true. Wolfram had given Juanita the task of planting explosives inside the missiles.

His assignment – incorporate bulk quantities of C4 into available cavities, under the launcher cradles to propagate the detonation.

Reluctantly, Kinsey agreed. "But, no matter what, the first smell of trouble you come over that stern."

They worked out an arrangement for their getaway. It centered on the diving sled and depended on their making connections again in the pitch dark of relatively deep water at night. The whole scheme seemed flimsy, but it was all they had.

"It'll be all right," she said. "They'll be busy on the foredeck pulling up their anchor and doing whatever they have to do to leave."

"They'd better be." He switched on a pencil flashlight. "Let's go over these missiles again."

In the tiny circle of light she unrolled Wolfram's drawings of details of the SSN-2A. "Wolfram says these are the solid fuel boosters. They fire first and then get jettisoned after the bird is flying." She pointed out a feature. "Hugo said the sustainer motor might be critical."

"Why?"

"He said even the sabotaged boosters might thrust the missile aloft enough to get it flying while the ship itself blows up."

"But there wouldn't be any guidance input," he said. "The thing would fly itself out of fuel and fall harmlessly."

"Or into houses on shore. Or onto an accomplice."

"Odds are against it."

"So, what do you think?"

Kinsey bit his lip. He didn't like making these decisions. "Okay. I say the first priority is getting charges into the boosters. After that, *if* there's time, and *if* sailors aren't racing around the decks, and *if* you can manage it, put charges into the sustainer motors. But boosters first."

They buckled on their heavy belts and, keeping their bodies below the gunwales, crawled like awkward seals from the cabin to the open deck.

Quickly they pushed the diving sled up and rolled it over the side. It splashed nose first into the water with a soft plunk. Then, equipment clanking, they rolled themselves over the side and down into the blackness.

The Komar's captain marked the fall of darkness with growing excitement. He glanced at the illuminated clock on the helm console. One more hour before his vessel would weight anchor and take the tide out of Freeport.

He ordered the bridge lights switched on and then once again pulled out the large chart of these waters.

"Call the first mate to the bridge."

"Aye, sir." The helmsman transmitted the order through the speaker system. A minute later the first mate appeared from below.

"Everything in order?"

"All correct, sir."

"Good." He pointed at the chart. "When we leave port, keep your speed well down." He pointed out a southerly route. "Keep a sharp lookout for bunkering moorings in here. We almost collided with one coming in."

"Very well, sir."

The captain glanced at his watch. The hour had arrived when he was authorized to tell the mate where they were going.

"I suppose you're as curious about this voyage as I am."

"I admit it, sir."

"Well, I don't know all of it, but, I do know our course and what we are to do. First, your course out of the harbor will be 215 degrees toward to Great Isaac Light." He described the rest of the route, the varying speeds, the requirements for the crew. By the end of it, the first mate and the mutely listening helmsman were as excited as the captain. And as mystified.

The diving sled dragged them through the inky waters in a straight line to the warship. Above them now, its own lights silhouetted it, a dark, huge wedge against the lighter surface. Juanita switched off the sled's electric motor and let it settle to rest on the smooth sand bottom, just below midship.

The two of them swam up to inspect the bottom of the ship with a red-masked torch. The ship had a relatively wide beam for its length, nearly twenty feet, with only a slight taper toward the stern. Close to the hull now, they could feel the beat of the ship's service diesel and hear the scrape and muffled thud of activity on board.

At the stern they saw what gave the vessel its speed – four propellers, each linked, they knew, to a twelve-hundred-horsepower diesel in the hull. Juanita and Kinsey had discussed the propellers. They had agreed they were the greatest menace, for after the ship weighed anchor, they would be started, and their churning, even at harbor speeds, would create a tide of their own – death for anyone caught in it.

Juanita swam carefully around the rudder. Kinsey, just below her, dragged the ladder

203

apparatus. Sacks of explosives attached to each of them floated like black jellyfish.

The boarding depended on binding a short magnesium ladder, with a pivot device at one end, flat against the rudder. Actually, it was the pivot device that was tied to the rudder, for the objective was, at the proper moment, to swing the ladder in a 180-degree arc to an upright position above the surface, parallel to the ship's transom. The ladder then would become a kind of extension of the rudder above water.

They worked swiftly in the faint illumination, hoping that the bubbles from their air exhaust would not be seen by the sentry above. In six minutes, they had affixed the ladder to the rudder and assured themselves that the pivot worked freely. Then they drifted silently to the harbor floor twelve feet below to wait for some sign from the gangway area.

They sat in the stygian depths like children on a beach, holding hands, watching the dull silver surface and the vast, morose shadow of the ship. From time to time Kinsey checked the luminous dial of his underwater watch. Their double tanks would give them enough air for well over an hour, especially if they did not exert themselves any more. Even if they exhausted the first tanks, there were spares with the sled. Another hour, if necessary.

Already it was high tide. It seemed unlikely the captain would miss a chance to sail in deep water through the treacherous shoals on the outside. Wolfram had predicted a departure in darkness to minimize the chances of aircraft interdiction.

So they waited.

Sixteen minutes had passed when they felt the vibration of a klaxon from above. He squeezed her hand hard. They heard more sounds, grating noises like wire hawsers rasping through pullies. They saw the sharply etched shadow of the gangway swing and move.

Juanita reached for Kinsey's arm and clutched it. Fumbling in the darkness, he helped her unhitch her tanks and lead belt. After making certain her sack of explosives was in place, he unslung his own and put it around her.

Lastly, he took her mouthpiece in his hands, and she floated toward the surface.

The clatter and thump of activity from the ship was startlingly loud. Abrupt commands in Arabic sounded through a loudspeaker. There were less dramatic shouts and calls on the foredeck.

Juanita pulled her mask down to dangle from her neck. Then she swung the ladder around until the pivot arrangement locked in place. The stern of the ship was still cloaked in darkness made stark by the brightly illuminated bow area.

Rung by rung she pulled herself up beside the transom and, head tilted, peeked through a maze of angle irons and equipment at the place where the sentry had been.

He was standing. His white blouse seemed like a beacon against the darker shadows of the superstructure. His back was to her, and he was moving forward toward the bow, ducking and scrambling under the low-hanging launcher tubes.

The twin launchers created two parallel walls for a roofless room. The third wall was the tarpaulin-covered storage rack for the Styx missiles, their stubby delta wings pushing conelike dents in the sides of the canvas covering. The deck was jammed with equipment to convey the missiles to the breeches of the launchers.

Juanita swung onto the deck. Crouching in the deeper shadows she went directly to the tarpaulin mass. The covering was held in place by lock snaps. As Juanita went to work in the darkness to unfasten them, there was a loud banging of metal against metal

206

from the foredeck. The gangway was being brought on deck and stowed. More orders barked over the loudspeaker.

She had opened the tarpaulin now and exposed the round metallic exhaust ports of the boosters. In the dim reflected light they glowed like ominous, deadly eyes. Each vent was sealed with an anticontamination lid, affixed tightly like the lid of a paint can. when fired, the enormous pressure of the rocket exhaust would blast them away. In the meantime they prevented seawater and damp air from intruding into the soild fuel propellant inside.

To pull these off, Wolfram had given her a clawed device made of brass to prevent dangerous sparks, but each cap would have to be replaced again as it was found.

From the foredeck came a new sound, the harsh grind of winches and the clank of chain. Good God! she thought. They're hoisting the anchor already. They hadn't expected the ship's work to proceed so speedily.

Feverishly, she hooked the brass claw into a seal on one of the topmost missiles and pried it away. The metal lid fell with a clatter to the deck and rolled under some equipment.

She froze. Had they heard it?

She zipped open the shoulder bag and retrieved one of the plastic-wrapped C4 loaves. Now, detonators!

Her fingers suddenly felt feeble, her hands shook. Two, Wolfram had said, over and over again. Two detonators per loaf. Angrily, she stabbed the copper cylinders through the plastic and then stuffed the charge well into the booster opening.

Now, replace the seal. One half of her seemed to issue the calm, methodical orders, the other half trembled. Where *was* the seal? She dropped to her hands and knees and groped around frantically in the dark for the flat lid.

Ahh! Here!

She stood quickly, squeezed the lid back into place, and rapped it with the heel of her hand all around the rim. Had she scratched the paint? It was impossible to see in this miserable light. Would they notice anything?

Never mind that. Get to the other seal on the second missile. At that moment there was a shudder through the ship and a heavy throbbing under her feet. Diesels!

Her stomach knotted. The ship's propulsion engines were turning. There was no time left now for the other missiles. She backed away from the grim mouths of the missiles.

Quickly now! Everything as it was! Careful. *Careful!* She pulled the tarpaulin into place and, making sure she got them in sequence, resnapped the fasteners.

The ship seemed to lurch slightly. Was it moving?

Not yet. Merely floating freely, relieved of its leash of anchor line. No time to lose now.

She stumbled back toward the stern and cracked her knee painfully against a jutting section of a launcher. She fell but continued scrambling toward the transom.

The ship was swinging now!

Her bag hooked on another projection, and she yanked at it. It wouldn't do to leave *that* bit of evidence behind. There was a ripping sound as it came loose. She hoped to God that none of the plastic loaves would fall out.

At the transom she reached for the ladder. A faint froth of water rose from the slowly beating propellers. Were they in forward or reverse? She looked to shore for a sign. One step into the wake of reversed propellers and her feet would be yanked into the thrashing blades.

She scrambled onto the ladder and down to the water. At the surface she slipped one foot gingerly into the froth. There was faint pushaway from the stern. Good, she thought. The engines are still in forward.

She pulled her face mask into place, then dropped into the dark water, clinging to the rudder post with her left arm. With her free hand she extracted her knife from its leg sheath and slashed the nylon lines that bound the ladder and pivot to the rudder blade. It fell free and slowly drifted toward the bottom.

Now, dive! Get away from those props!

Summoning all of her strength she plunged down past the white foam of the propeller wash, down into the blackness. To her left she saw a faint red dot. She swam toward it with renewed strength and collided with Kinsey in the watery darkness. An instant later she felt something punch against her mouth, her respirator. Gratefully, she bit into it and began breathing while Kinsey fumbled to hook her tanks back over her shoulders and hang her weight belt around her waist.

Above them there was a gush of silver and gold bubbles bouncing off the harbor lights like some vertical waterfall on the surface. Turning in an arc toward the main channel and the sea, the huge shadow of the ship pulled away.

17

Although Wolfram was more exasperated than distressed to learn that Hamir had been irradiated mortally by one of the emir's devices, it was a serious complication.

"It's pure circumstance, Hugo. Who could have known?" Hamir's skin was waxen. The radiation seemed to have melted weight from him.

The two of them sat in easy chairs in a specially segregated room of Walter Reed Hospital. It was now 9 P.M.

"In fact, Hugo," Hamir smiled thinly, "it is something of a release, you know? After all, how many of us get such precise data on their mortality?"

"How long do they give you?"

"They don't know exactly. Depends what degree of dosage I got, of course. Based on the length of time of exposure and my condition now, a few more days of relative freedom marked by some increased frequency of stomach and intestinal distress. Then, rapidly downhill."

Wolfram nodded. "Meanwhile, my guess

is that our man will be en route to Washington, appearing soon – two to three days."

"I want to help."

"Nonsense! You've done it all."

"Sit here? Wait for the angel?" Hamir's laugh turned into a snarl. "This is one corpse, Hugo, who wants to put a dead hand on the throat of his killer."

Wolfram had hoped for as much. Even a dying Hamir could perform a valuable recognition function.

After a moment Hamir asked, "What are they doing about security, Hugo?"

"Trying to be inconspicuous. There's a very real problem in this situation of panic in the streets. If the press gets wind of this, it would be like the bubonic plague."

They sat in silence for a time. Wolfram stared at his hands. He really wanted to leave, check further on the security network. He was convinced that the FBI, the Secret Service, and the other agencies harbored a deep skepticism about the whole business.

Except for Hamir's situation, Wolfram was unable to offer them anything but speculation – not an adequate description of the man they were to watch for, or even that he was definitely the man. Nor could he provide them with a plausible basis for his speculations. The domestic agencies were to be kept in the dark about what had happened at Ishbaad. Even within the Company there was only one man who knew, and he had the information only sketchily from the Chairman himself.

Following the usual pattern, the Company and the two domestic agencies were bickering over their respective jurisdictions. Legally, of course, the Company had absolutely no authority to so much as make a face at the emir inside the United States.

And then, there was the State Department, and a serious foreign policy argument. The emir was unfriendly to the United States, said State. Still, there could be no affront to him that could be interpreted as an anti-Arab gesture. Very touchy, said State. The magic word – oil.

"Washington," Hugo muttered.

"What's the matter?" asked Hamir.

"Security problems."

"They don't really believe there's a danger, do they?"

Wolfram sighed. "Yes and no. This town takes menace for granted, like smog – it won't kill you, until it kills you."

"We're wasting our time then – whatever time we have, that is."

"Oh, no," Wolfram said quickly. "We'll get him."

He didn't believe if for a minute.

The atomic energy expert studied Wolfram for a moment. Then he removed one of the harmless cobalt pens from his vest pocket and laid it on the desk between them.

"Mr. Wolfram, under agency standards the maximum permissible dosage of gamma radiation to the whole body is thirty roentgens a year." Dr. Atkinson tapped the pen with his forefinger. "One of these, treated in a nuclear reactor to become the isotope cobalt 60, would emit that much radiation in a fraction of a second. Just walking into a small room where there was one would be extremely hazardous. Touching one would be fatal, unquestionably."

"I understand that, doctor. My question is, how would an individual handle not just one, but dozens of them?"

"If he wanted to live, the pens would have to have substantial shielding. Lead would be best."

"How much lead?"

"It would depend how far from the source he would be."

"Explain."

"Radiation disperses, like light. The

amount of radiation is inversely proportional to the square of the distance from the source. In other words, at a distance of two feet there would be only one-quarter the radiation at one foot, at three feet one-ninth, and so on."

"And the lead?"

"For cobalt 60 a half-inch of lead shielding would cut the radiation in half. Each additional half-inch would further halve the radiation. With about four inches of lead, there would be virtually no gamma rays penetrating."

"Suppose a man wants to safely infiltrate one of these pens into a – room. What would he need?"

The agency man took a small notebook from his pocket. Using the emir's pen he sketched a diagram.

"One thing is certain," he said. "He couldn't do it surreptitiously. At the very least he would need a thick-walled lead box of some kind to carry his material."

"And when he opened the box?"

"His clothing would have to be lead-shielded. He'd need tongs to put distance between himself and the cobalt. Then he would have to make a very rapid departure."

Wolfram drummed his fingers on the desk. "How much does a cubic inch of lead weight?"

The doctor extracted a small book of tables from his pocket. "Point-four of a pound."

"That would mean one hell of a heavy box if it had four-inch walls."

"The walls wouldn't have to be that thick," the agency man told him. "There are precautions that could be taken to expose him to a relatively safe level of dosage – distance, for example. If he kept himself three feet away from the source he would reduce his factor of exposure by nearly ninety percent, not counting any reduction by shielding. He could use a much lighter box."

"A yard," Wolfram mused. "Awkward."

"Not really," said Atkinson. "Our people regularly manipulate dangerous materials at that distance and farther. You see, distance is the greatest protection against dangerous radiation. Take cobalt 60, for example. An amount that would give you a fatal dose in ten minutes at ten inches wouldn't give you a fatal dose in ten months at ten feet."

"But still, to handle, move it. A lead box would be difficult."

"Well, it could be constructed for easy handling. Wheels, that kind of thing. And, of course, the lead container wouldn't need a lead bottom. Radiation would all be downward."

Wolfram pulled at his earlobe. "I suppose it could be done with the right cover. He could pose as a workman – a painter. Perhaps a plumber."

It was midnight in the security agency's operations room.

"Your call is coming in, sir."

"Thank you, sergeant."

Wolfram reached across his console table to pick up a headset and threw the lighted connection switch. "How did it go?"

Kinsey's voice echoed through the satellite system as if from outside a metal drum. "A mixed performance."

"Did you get on board?"

"Juanita went up. We were a little late getting there. They had security on watch until just before they hauled anchor."

"Was she able to plant any charges?"

"She fixed one SSN-2A. Barely. There wasn't any time to do the others."

"I didn't think you'd get anything. Describe the missile arrangement for me."

Kinsey explained what Juanita had found, how she had slipped a double charge into one of the Styx missiles on the top tier.

"That means we have a fifty-fifty chance of getting the Komar before it gets a bird in the air."

"Or a fifty-fifty chance of *not* getting the Komar."

"That's why we have to keep on top of this. Have you gotten a report from the navy yet?"

"That's the bad news," said Kinsey. "They think they've lost the ship."

"What do you mean, *think?*"

"The Komar left the harbor, but turned east toward the Atlantic instead of west toward Florida. They didn't expect that. Now the Komar could be any one of some twenty-three vessels in the New Providence channel."

"By now the Komar could have doubled back and be on its way to Florida."

"Possible."

"Much traffic in the Gulf Stream?"

"Jammed. Everything from yachts to supertankers. They all make the same kind of blip on the big screen."

"And the Komar would probably only make freighter speed in order to avoid attracting attention."

"Right."

Wolfram stared hard at the big glass panel map of the Florida straits. "So we probably have a missile ship somewhere off the coast. But where? Key Biscayne? Miami?

218

Lauderdale? Palm Beach? They're all within easy range of the Komar.

"What are your instructions?"

"There's nothing more you can do there. You and Juanita fly on up here." Wolfram told him where to report and then broke the connection.

There were more than a hundred miles of coastline in the target area, all of it virtually unmonitored, unguarded. To find a single ship, let alone a man, in the dark of night was to search blindfolded in a titanic haystack for the proverbial needle.

18

The panel truck rolled slowly along the empty boulevard, past deserted bars and grills, past the shuttered orange juice stands and coral shops until it reached the turnoff.

There is a chill, the driver mused, in these hours before dawn when the city seems more dead than asleep. He shivered, recited a prayer.

The narrow road he turned off on led around the rim of the harbor toward a marina. Ranks of expensive white motorboats nuzzled at pilings. On a main trunk pier, beside a small building glowing with lights, a handful of men stood talking.

At the end of the pier a boat engine roared into life and then throttled back. The cluster of men moved toward the sound, their rubber soles thudding on the wooden planking.

The truck driver pulled into the marina parking area and sat watching them. He waited patiently until they climbed into their fishing craft and cast off.

After they had gone, he climbed out of the truck and made his way to the marina building. Behind a counter inside, a round-faced man in a khaki shirt with the name "Herb" embroidered over the pocket was scribbling something on a tablet.

"Good morning."

"Hi."

"I'm Al Mazer. I've got a boat reserved."

"Right. You're the underwater picture man."

"That's me."

"Well, she's all ready."

"My associates have already paid up and all that, right."

"Everything is A-OK." Herb went to a window and pointed. "She's the third one over."

"Twin engines?"

"That's what you ordered, that's what you got." He smiled. "Sure you wouldn't like to try a little fishing?"

"If I want a fish, I'll hit one with my camera." The two men laughed.

"Right. Need any help with your gear?"

"No. I have a hand truck to wheel it around, but I might use one of your davits to lower the gear on board, if I may."

"Help yourself."

"Thanks."

"Say, you want to be careful diving out there alone."

"I do it all the time. Problem is, if you get too many divers on the scene, you spook the fish. No fish, no pictures."

"I guess so. Which reef you going to?"

Mazer pointed to the open chart of the area on an end wall. "That one."

"Deep water there. Around a hundred feet."

"No problem. I watch my time carefully, take it slow coming back up."

"You're the boss. At least you divers don't lose anchors like the fishermen do sometimes."

"No way."

It took Mazer fifteen minutes and three trips to roll all of his equipment to the boat and stow it aboard. At the end he double-checked to make sure that all was in order – the ropes and pulleys, sheet steel "camera" chests, smaller containers, tool kit, diving components, special heavy gloves.

Everything in place, he started the boat engines and let them warm up. The smell of exhaust mingled with the damp harbor odors exhilarated him. For a moment he stood silent looking across the dark harbor. Then he cast off.

The Komar ran without light at twenty knots. In the moonless sky, the horizon to the west glowed with the aura of Florida's Gold Coast some forty miles away.

On the bridge the captain marked the time on the ship's chronometer.

"Set your course at 280 degrees, helmsman."

"Aye, sir."

The captain turned to his first officer. "Forty-seven minutes to go. Have the asbestos screens been secured over the sterns of the launchers?"

"All secure, sir."

"Very well." Those screens are a complication, he thought. But, he supposed, they would muffle the flash of the boosters enough to limit attention from other ships in the area. "What does radar show, number one?"

"Two ships in the area, a northbound freighter and a southbound tanker."

"Will they be close by at firing?"

"We calculate the freighter will be thirteen miles to port and the tanker will be eleven miles to starboard."

"If those screens work, they shouldn't raise any problem for us. Have there been any signals?"

"None."

"All's well, then. We proceed."

The Komar completed its turning arc toward the west.

Outside the inlet he opened up the twin engines. The motorboat pounded across the calm, dark sea, its tachometers pressing dangerously close to their red lines. Each small swell on the surface hammered against the keel. The craft yawed and lurched, its propellers whining at empty air before biting back again into the water.

Mazer clutched the wheel, knees flexed to absorb the pounding against his feet, his eyes fixed on the compass needle fluttering around the ninety-degree mark. From time to time he checked his watch.

After some six minutes of wide-open

running, he throttled the engines back to eight hundred rpm and switched on the illuminated depth gauge. As the boom of his engine faded, his ears picked up the sound of a whistle buoy a mile to the north of him.

The gauge put the water here at more than two hundred feet. It was one of the trenches between the reefs that parallel the Florida coast, four hundred to six hundred yards apart. He scanned the horizon for other small craft but saw none.

He studied the gauge carefully. It held at the two-hundred-foot mark for a time and then began to flutter. Gradually, the orange light began to oscillate into a shallower range as the ocean floor angled upward toward the reef line. One-twenty, one-ten, a hundred. He lowered his speed still more until the boat was barely making headway. Ninety-five feet.

He turned the boat to a north-south line, following the underwater ridge, and moved to the stern. Quickly, he snapped open one of the smaller cases and removed from it a dull black cube about the size of a transistor radio. Attached to the cube were a small float, a hundred-foot nylon line, and a lead anchor. From the top of the tube he pulled a telescoped aerial. Next to the aerial was a switch held fast by a retaining pin.

He pulled the pin, flicked the switch, and placed the items on the sea surface. He watched anxiously as the box with its float bobbed in the wake of the propellers while the line and anchor speared downward. As distance widened between the boat and the device, he saw it right itself, aerial up.

He returned to the cabin to check his depth. Still over the reef. Again he scurried to the back of the boat and repeated the process with the second black cube, then the third, and the fourth.

He let the boat continue on up the reef line until he had a good hundred yards between himself and the nearest aerial. Shutting down the engine, he went to the bow and cast the anchor over the side. He checked his watch.

Seventeen minutes to spare.

The captain of the Komar tried to keep excitement out of his voice. "Order action stations, number one."

The first officer pressed a large red button on the bridge console. "Action stations! Action stations!" he shouted into the speaker system.

The coastal glow was brighter now. The captain scanned the horizon with his night glasses. The two far-off ships were visible in their proper channels. From the deck below came the sounds of crewmen running to the forward turret.

The intercom crackled. "Fire control ready!"

"Fire control ready," the first officer repeated to the captain.

"Very well. Stand by."

The captain watched the chronometer on the console. "Reduce speed to five knots, number one."

The officer shouted the order into the intercom. The pitch and roll of the ship subsided.

"Prepare to fire missiles one and two?"

Again the first officer transmitted the order, and a moment later the response came back.

"One and two are ready, sir."

The captain squinted at the chronometer. Seconds ticked by as the ship's crew stood frozen at their posts.

"On the mark!"

"Mark!"

The captain took a deep breath. "Five. Four. Three. Two. One. *Fire one!*"

"*Fire one!*"

The night suddenly was split by a giant wedge of yellow flame.

Eighteen miles to the west Al Mazer spotted a twinkle of light on the horizon.

"Bravo!" he said aloud. Soon he would know whether the electronic homing system worked as accurately as he had planned. A fraction of degree of variance and his boat, instead of one of the floating black boxes, could be the point of impact. In ninety seconds he would know.

He watched the horizon for the expected second wink of light.

"What?" Instead of a wink, there was a flash like an orange blossom. In an instant it was replaced by tiny spots of light, like sparks.

Mazer put his hands to his face and sobbed. What went wrong? A bungled loading? A breakdown of the launcher itself? A faulty booster? All the work. All the planning –"

Something made him look up again. A tiny, distant finger of light scratched at the surface of the ocean and moved rapidly toward him. In a millisecond a black, arrow shape plunged into the sea, skipped once like a flat rock, and then disappeared in a huge geyser of water a hundred feet high. A loud slap of sound struck his ears. It was followed by the thud and hiss of the trailing sound waves.

"It *worked!*" he shrieked.

He clung to the gunwales of the motorboat as waves of water from the impact shook it. The missile had homed directly on the nearest black box.

He went to the bow, pulled up the anchor, and then took the boat to the impact area. As he approached, he could see the black box still bobbing on the surface, its aerial swinging like a ship. That's a bit of luck, he thought. His homing beacon was not so precise that the missile hit it. The aerial would be a handy marker.

He cruised on past the homing device and picked up each of the others. Then he returned and anchored over the impact area. Nothing more could be done now until daylight.

Wolfram napped in his chair by the console in the security room.

A duty officer nudged him. "Wake up, sir. We have a mesage that might interest you."

"What have you got?"

"The Coast Guard says they received signals from two ships off Florida. Both reported sighting what they thought was an explosion. Either a ship or a plane."

"Where off Florida?"

The officer went to the glass panel. "One ship was here. The other was here."

"That would put this explosion about twenty miles off Hillsboro Inlet."

"That's about right.

"That's the one we're looking for." He glanced at the wall clock. "What time did it happen?"

"A little over two hours ago."

"Two *hours!*" Wolfram snapped. "What the hell took them so long to report it?"

"It seems the navy – or our people – neglected to bring the Coast Guard into the mission. So the Coast Guard took the report and dispatched a cutter, but they didn't buck the information along. Anyhow, the navy finally caught up with the radio chatter and –"

"For God's sake," Wolfram rasped.

Nevertheless, it was the signal he needed. At last they had pinned down their adversary to a time and a place.

But that delay!

How long did it take to get from Florida to Washington?

A commercial jet could do it in two hours.

Mazer hauled himself to his feet and stretched his arms and legs against his taut diving suit. A hundred feet below it would still be a deep blue twilight, but the water was crystal clear. He knew what he was looking for, and where.

He attached his pulleys to the gunwale, tightened the wingnuts, and then threaded one end of the long nylon line through the double docks. He shouldered himself into the heavy tanks, hooked a weighted belt around his middle. Across his chest he clipped a canvas bag containing key wrenches, pliers, some metering devices, and a small acetylene torch in case any cutting had to be done.

Retrieving the pulley end of the rope, he looped it into a smaller pulley on one of the sheet steel chests and dropped the box over the side. It quickly filled with water and faded into the depths with the nylon line following it. The other end of the long line he tied to his belt.

He donned his leaden gloves and flexed his fingers, pulled his face mask into place, and bit on his mouthpiece.

Finally, after one last look around, he tumbled backward into the sea and followed the nylon line down through the thickening blue of the depths. Near the bottom, the underwater world suddenly brightened again with light reflected from white sand and coral. When he touched down he looked around for the missile's distinctive shape.

There! Fifty yards from his anchor line, wedged into a declivity, was the Styx. The body was at a sixty-degree angle.

Mazer swam toward the aft end of the missile. All seemed in order. He took the line from his belt and hitched it around the missile in front of the wing. From his chest bag he removed a small Geiger counter and took a reading.

Virtually nothing.

He swam back to the chest on the bottom under the boat and brought it back to the nose cone. Then, astride the missile body itself, he began the delicate work of unfastening the air shield with the key wrenches. In three minutes he had freed the magnesium shield. It rolled away on the gently sloping bottom.

He took another reading. The levels were slightly higher now, but within the safety margin. From his chest bag he took an angled mirror, like a dentist's, and inspected the inside of the missile cavity. Not a dent. Not a stripped thread. No broken seals.

Holding the mirror in one hand, his free hand darted into the cavity, grasped a handle, and pulled forth an extremely heavy cylinder measuring $4\frac{1}{2}$ inches in diameter and 6¼ inches long. He thrust the cylinder into the brackets inside the steel chest, fastened a retaining clamp, closed the chest lid, and slipped its lock snaps shut.

Another reading – everything was still within the safety margin. Tungsten was a far better radiation shield than lead. It was heavier, but had less bulk for the same protection.

Now he untied the line from the missile and swam with it back under the boat. He hauled against the pulleys until the steel chest with its sixty-pound cylinder inside bumped across the bottom toward him like a reluctant pendulum.

He ascended slowly to allow extra time for decompression. It wouldn't do for the bends to interrupt the mission at this stage.

At the dock Herb took the bowline and helped Mazer onto the dock.

"Well, how'd she go?"

"The boat was fine," Mazer smiled. "Got just what I wanted."

"Lots of pictures?"

"Sure." Mazer pointed at the dock davit. "Say, would you haul that chest up for me? I'm wrung out. I stowed all of my stuff in it, so be gentle."

"Okay."

Mazer walked to his vehicle and removed the hand truck from the back. From a distance he watched as Herb worked the heavy chest up and deposited it on the dock.

He'll be all right, Mazer thought. There's not enough radiation coming out of that to kill a fly. He rolled the hand truck back to the dock, but kept well back from the chest.

"Listen, you're a big help to a tired man, Herb." He stuffed a five-dollar bill into the man's shirt pocket. "Would you mind wheeling that thing up to the truck for me? I'll unload the other stuff."

"Sure 'nough." Herb nudged the hand truck under the box and levered it up. "You got some heavy cameras there."

"A couple of underwater specials."

"Gee, I'd love to see them."

Mazer looked at his watch. "I really don't have much time, Herb. I've got to process that film and get it delivered. I'm on a deadline."

19

A mockingbird trilled inside the fan-shaped leaf cluster of a palmetto. Harada brought his glasses up and tried to focus on the bird. All he picked up was a blur of gray feathers and green foliage. His glasses were far too powerful for birdwatching.

Everglades bush obscured the entourage heading his way from the parking lot, but he could hear the far-off clumping of feet and the hum of voices near the beginning of the bird sanctuary's boardwalk trail.

Just ahead of the group there was a relatively open space in the vegetation. He leaned down, elbows steady against the wooden railing, and focused across the open area two hundred yards away.

A figure moved through the field of vision – one of the guards. Then came some other individuals, some of them obviously American security men, then the official party – a State Department official, a translator, a guide in the uniform of the bird sanctuary. Beside him, in a dress uniform, headdress, dark glasses was the emir. Or was it?

Harada sharpened the focus. The figure seemed to be only a few feet away, lips moving inside the black beard. Hands gestured.

The face *could* be the emir's. Harada thought. He watched closely. The uniformed figure stepped along. More gestures, a broad smile, a laugh.

This was not the emir. The hands turned too languorously. There was no authority in them, no snap in the figure's movements. The walk was different.

A good likeness, but it wasn't the real thing.

The stand-in could have fooled a detective, perhaps even a camera, but he would never fool a professional actor.

Harada restored his binoculars to their case and walked rapidly around the board-walk complex toward the sanctuary's souvenir shop and a telephone.

The panel truck pulled around to the rear of the big motel in West Palm Beach and parked beside a green van with Ohio license plates.

The driver climbed down from his truck and looked around. Taking a set of keys from

235

his pocket, he found one that would unlock the van. He opened it and fumbled under the front seat until his fingers closed around a room key. He pocketed the key and opened the sliding door of the van to inspect the interior.

The wall of tungsten shielding was in place between the driver's seat and the back. He opened the back door of his truck and then went in search of an assistant. Beside the swimming pool of the motel, he found a young man pulling fallen palm fronds from the water.

"Say, pal, would you give me a hand moving some stuff? I got a back sprain, and it just kills me to lift."

"I got a lot of work to do here."

Mazer smiled and tucked a bill into his shirt front. "It'll only take a minute."

"I'll make some time."

Mazer led him to the truck. "Just move that heavy metal box over into the green van, will you? I can handle the lighter stuff."

"I see you do some diving."

"Yeah. A little."

"You want me to move that stuff, too?"

"No. I'll take care of it."

He stood well back as the young man, grunting, hefted the steel trunk. "Don't tip it over. There's some material inside that could spill."

The young man staggered to the van with the metal case and deposited it on the floor. "Man, what you got in there? Rocks?"

Mazer laughed. "Would you believe the keys to the world's future?"

"Sorry," the pool attendant grinned. "If that's the future, it's too heavy for me." He waved a goodbye and went back to his chores at the pool.

Mazer retrieved an overnight bag from the truck and went to the room for which he had the key. Inside, he entered the bathroom and stared at the somewhat unfamiliar face in the mirror.

From his kit he removed a bottle of peroxide. With a cotton swab he rapidly daubed the chemical into his cropped hair. Slowly it turned the color of brass. More chemical and it turned white. After applying the chemical to his eyebrows and lashes, he took a tiny plastic contact lens box from the kit, put the lenses on the tip of his finger, and worked them into place.

Finally, he looked over the documents again – a driver's license, press credentials in English, French, and German, a passport. The name on the passport was Heinz Jaeger.

They met that afternoon around an oval table in one of the beige conference rooms of the State Department. An assistant secretary of state presided.

"The most urgent matter at this time, then," he said, "is that we adopt a coherent procedure to cope with what may or may not be an overt threat."

Wolfram, bone tired, sat in a chair by the wall outside the circle of active participants. There on the sufferance of the Company, he had been enjoined not to speak, except to answer a direct question. Even then, he was to offer the two Company officials an opportunity to answer for him.

The State Department executive continued. "It has been suggested that the emir of Al Hakeer, now visiting in Florida, is carrying out a scheme against our national interests. It further has been suggested that we preempt this scheme, abort it, if you will, by detaining the emir. The rationale for this extreme move is that the emir is *not* the emir, but a double, and that detaining him would quickly expose the fact that dirty work is afoot.

"Speaking of my own department, I can only reflect the position that we are *not* in possession of enough facts to warrant such
238

a diplomatically dangerous move." He looked around the table.

"Our feeling is about the same as yours," said the FBI agent-in-charge. "All we have is speculation and the one fact of a guy who is dying from radiation."

"Exactly," said the Secret Service official. "We're not kissing this thing off. We're keeping our eyes and ears open, but then there may be a half-dozen more of these schemes cooking that we have to watch out for. The president is always a target."

The assistant secretary turned to the senior man from the Company. "I guess the ball's in your court, Harvey. Where do we stand?"

The Company's man cleared his throat. "Well, as you know, we have certain inputs. I'm not going to play the record for you again *in toto,* but what we know tends to confirm the intelligence that Mr. Wolfram here first reported."

The assistant secretary raised an eyebrow. "Maybe I missed something. Just what do we have?"

The Company's man shifted uneasily. "Well, there was this business of the boat blowing up this morning in the Gulf Stream. We were informed, reliably, that such a thing might happen and that it was part of this emir's scheme."

"But what does it all *mean*, Harvey?" the assistant secretary pressed. "Does the Company have something it hasn't told the rest of us?"

Harvey frowned. "You have everything that we have."

"Perhaps," said the assistant secretary, "Mr. – ah, Wolfram is it? – can help us?"

"How it came about is immaterial, gentlemen," Wolfram told them. "The fact is that the threat is real."

"Why should we give your say-so credence?" the FBI man asked. "And, by the way, just who are you, Mr. Wolfram?"

"Mr. Wolfram is a consultant to us," Harvey interjected hastily. "His information is reliable."

"That doesn't tell us anything," the FBI man snapped.

"It's not supposed to!"

"Gentlemen, gentlemen," the assistant secretary said. "Let's not bicker. We're here to develop a procedure, if any is needed."

The others stared at their pads.

"Now then," the assistant secretary went on, "we are agreed that there can be no overt action in this matter."

"Why not?" said the Secret Service representative. "If someone moves against the president, we'll bounce him. It's a crime."

"It's an *embarrassment,*" replied the State Department's man. "Can you imagine if our authorities jailed an Arab prince?" He shook his head. "Besides, our policy forbids open action. This meeting is merely to review procedures to implement it."

"So what else can we do?" asked the FBI's man. "We have key points under surveillance, radiometers spotted at all of the ports of entry into the U.S. The Secret Service has tight security around the White House. We can't set up road blocks without bringing the state and local police in."

"Besides," the Secret Service representative added, "who the hell are we looking for?"

"It is humanly impossible to cover all of the access to this city even when the police and military are on board," the FBI man observed. "And they aren't." He brought his fist down on the table. "We're doing our best, but dammit, if we can't go public we're chopping down most of our deterrent. That's a hell of a nonsensical risk to take to save the State Department some embarrassment."

"You must be joking! We're not just trying to outmaneuver some Arab prince

241

who may or may not mean us some harm. We're talking about Middle East *policy!*"

"I didn't know we had one," the FBI man muttered.

The assistant secretary flushed. "That's enough of that." He looked around the table. "Let me cite some facts. One, the secretary of state backs our policy view without reservation. Two, the White House backs the secretary.

"We must be pragmatic. The Company has come into possession of certain information by God knows what means, but it is all based on supposition and speculation."

"What about the double for the emir?" asked the Company's man. "It does suggest, at the very least, that the emir is elsewhere."

"Oh, *come* now," the assistant secretary sniffed. "We have our own man with the emir at this very moment."

"How does he know it's the emir?" asked the FBI's man.

The assistant secretary scowled. "I think we're pushing this charade too far. Necessary precautions – yes. We'd do the same on any threat, foreign or domestic. But we shall not panic and gallop off in all directions."

"What direction *do* we gallop off in, Mr. Assistant Secretary?"

"Why don't we just let the egg hatch a bit,
242

gentlemen? Let's see what kind of a bird we've got." He smiled. "In the meantime, perhaps we should review again who is watching the nest. Now then."

The meeting went on for hours. At the end, nothing had changed except the time.

20

Twenty-four hours later Heinz Jaeger turned his green van off Interstate 95 south of Rocky Mount, North Carolina, and into a motel. The long but relaxing drive through the bleak coastal plains of Georgia, South Carolina, and North Carolina was precisely what he needed to compose himself for the next leg of his journey, a kind of mental decompression after the frustrating events of Friday.

As he motored the nearly five hundred miles from his overnight stop in Jacksonville, Florida, he had kept his ear tuned to the jangle of country music stations and waited in vain for the newscasts that might bring him some word regarding the Komar's fate. It bothered him only a little that he heard nothing. Perhaps the Coast Guard *was* treating it routinely. Even if there had been survivors, even if they had questioned them, what could they possible have learned? Something, perhaps, but something was not nearly enough.

After checking in, Jaeger parked his van in the slot next to his room. Automatically, he checked the small radiometer pinned inside his shirt. Nothing of significance. His shielding was working better than he had expected. He glanced toward the back of the van. The locked steel chest with its tungsten cylinder inside was secure.

From the forward area of the van he withdrew the cases containing his special camera and equipment. After locking the van securely, he wheeled the gear into his room on the hand truck.

Inside the room he basked for a moment in the cooled air and then showered and slipped into fresh clothes. At the bathroom mirror he inspected his hair and eyes. The face staring back at him still startled him.

He opened the large, heavy camera case and hauled out the huge box camera inside. To a casual observer it would have appeared to be made of rosewood, a kind of old-fashioned portrait camera. In fact, the wood was merely a veneer over a metal interior with a platinum shielding. Like other portrait cameras it had a long, telescoping black snout, the usual shutter and exposure fixtures, and a socket for a long remote control shutter cord.

But this was no camera. Its weight alone set it apart, for with the platinum liner, it weighed nearly fifty pounds. To support this heavy object Jaeger had a steel tripod. Each leg terminated in a ball-bearing caster. Even with the camera mounted on it, the tripod rolled easily.

Jaeger maneuvered the equipment, sighted through it at objects around the room. As he cocked and triggered the inner mechanism, he savored the smooth, oiled click of steel parts. He inspected the auxiliary equipment – a number of carbon dioxide cylinders and a set of long, accordion-hinged tongs that could be made even longer by screw-on handles. The tongs had a socket arrangement that fit onto the top of the tripod and allowed the assembly to be used as a kind of light crane to lift and move heavy objects from a safe distance.

Manipulating the tongs with surprising skill, Jaeger picked up small objects in the room, moved them around, turned them. But then, he had practiced with them for many, many months.

Almost reluctantly he restored the equipment to its cases. From his travel kit he withdrew a road map and studied it. Only two hundred and fifty miles to Washington.

All of them but Magraw met for dinner in a private room of one of Washington's downtown hotels. It hadn't been a successful meal. The presence of Hamir, the specter at the feast, was all too real.

In appearance, he did not strike them as too bad. His color was no worse, even though his eyes had the bright, almost drugged, glaze of one with a high fever. His hair was in place still. He suffered only modest discomfort, and, as a temporary expedient, he had had a transfusion of blood that afternoon.

"Actually," he told them, "the transfusion did me a world of good. I feel more or less normal, not overly weak. Even a little appetite."

The others knew it could well have been any of them counting out the final hours, and still might be.

Wolfram stood up. "I believe we have to do some serious rethinking about our friend the emir and what he's up to. We may be acting under a misconception as to the scope of the emir's target."

"What do you mean?" asked Kinsey.

"At the outset, you'll recall, Hamir determined that the emir holds a bitter enmity for the United States leadership, which he believes to be pro-Zionist, anti-Arab, et cetera.

"Naturally, when individuals, domestic or foreign, talk of the U.S. leadership, they mean the executive branch of government generally and the White House specifically. We assumed the same thing."

He looked around the table, then went on. "But what about Congress and the Supreme Court?"

"Do you mean to say that his target is all three branches of government?" Kinsey demanded.

"Why not? Enough pens could do the job. *One* pen could do the job if everyone was exposed to it."

"But does he have enough pens to go around?" asked Harada.

"Right," Kinsey noted. "He's only got a quarter of his original allotment, if that." He shook his head. "I don't buy it. Too many people."

"When the idea occurred to me, I had some serious reservations, too," said Wolfram. "So, this afternoon after Hamir got his transfusion, we went over all of the old tapes of the emir's speeches."

"And?"

Hamir answered. "The problem in translation always is that one has some preconception of what one is hearing. I heard some Arab words meaning *leaders,* and I heard and translated them as *leadership,* meaning, to me, the president. In fact, when we went back and listened to the speeches from the three-branch perspective, what the emir said fits as if tailored. He meant leadership very, very plurally. A *lot* of people."

"But how?" Juanita asked. "There are hundreds of these people. Besides, even if all four missiles had connected, could they carry that many pens?"

Harada took the emir's pen from his pocket and laid it on the dining table. "Not a large item, but not small if you want to carry many of them within a short-range missile warhead."

"I know, I know. And that problem's got me stumped. Each pen weighs twelve grams, about a half-ounce."

Kinsey jotted some figures on a napkin. "Five hundred plus would weigh in at about fifteen or sixteen pounds. I guess that's not an impossibility for four Styx missiles."

"Don't forget the safety shielding though," said Hamir. "Each pen would require three or four ounces of shielding at the very least."

"Right," said Wolfram. "Based on the maximum capacity of a Styx warhead, the most that could safely be handled in one missile would be thirty pens."

"It scarcely seems enough to implement a threat to the whole government," Harada observed.

"I agree," said Wolfram. "And as I said, it puzzles me."

"What are the security agencies doing about it?"

"They're watching the White House and the president. Period."

"So where does that leave us?" asked Kinsey.

"I can answer that," said Hamir. "We think, we plan, and we act as we must to stop this man. Whether he has thirty pens or thirty thousand, he is a dangerous killer."

"But where the hell *is* he? And when's he coming?"

21

Brilliant early fall sun set the white dome of the Capitol in sharp relief against the clear afternoon sky.

Standing on the east steps of the Capitol Plaza, Heinz Jaeger watched crowds of tourists ambling up and down the pyramidal steps. Less than an hour before he had driven the van into a motel just across the Potomac. He had retained a bellman to porter his cases of equipment to a room and then had taken a taxicab across the twin highway bridges, past the Jefferson Memorial, down Maryland Avenue to where he was now.

The day could not be better, he thought. The air was crystal – unusual for Washington – just on the edge of coolness. He took a deep breath and moved ahead. For the time being his mission was reconnaissance, checking details.

As he climbed the steps and entered through the main portico, he glanced upward into the yawning dome above. His eyes wandered across the frieze, then down to the giant painting of John Trumbull of the "Declaration of Independence."

Jaeger stood for a moment, then walked toward the House of Representatives. He scarcely glanced at the pseudo-Roman gallery of historic figures as he passed through Statuary Hall. Soon he came to the entry to the House cloakrooms.

A guard blocked his way. "I'm sorry, sir. This area is closed to the public."

"Yes. Of course." Jaeger rummaged through his pockets and produced a thick manila envelope, from which he took some documents. "As you can see, I've been authorized to come into the House tonight to photograph the chamber. Also the Senate. I thought I'd have a quick look first to see if there's any problem that I haven't anticipated. Extra equipment, that kind of thing."

The officer studied the pages briefly. "Okay. I can let you in for a quick look now, but I'll have to stay with you."

Jaeger smiled. "I understand perfectly. This'll take two minutes. Maybe I'll get a fix on some power outlets, in case I opt for lights."

"Follow me, please." The guard led Jaeger all the way around the locked House chamber to the entrance to the Speaker's lobby. "You'll probably want to bring your equipment in this way, if you are taking your pictures from the floor of the House."

"Is that the best way?"

"I think so. Most of the power outlets are back here, if you need them." They went into a long, narrow room.

"Marvelous, marvelous," Jaeger muttered as he glanced at the ornate walls decorated with the gold-framed portraits of past Speakers of the House. There were a number of varished doors along one wall. The guard fumbled with keys until he found one that worked in the lock of one of the doors.

He waved Jaeger through into the huge, barely illuminated House chamber itself, silent and empty. Jaeger was facing the semicircular ranks of high-backed wooden pews where the members sat.

"It's going to be a problem," he told the guard.

"Umm," the officer agreed. "It's a big room."

"Do you know the dimensions by any chance?"

"It's a hundred and thirty-nine feet long and ninety-three feet wide."

Jaeger squinted. "For me that's a problem. I'll need extra time." He smiled quickly at the officer. "Time exposures, you see?"

252

"I see."

He glanced upward. "I think the best bet will be to shoot from the galleries."

Holding hands like honeymooners, Juanita and Kinsey roamed the lower levels of the Capitol only a few hundred yards and one floor from the House chamber. Each wore a shoulder bag from which a cord extended to ear pieces. They might have been listening to taped lectures. Actually, the bags contained radiometers. Alert for the telltale staccato clicks of gamma radiation, they heard only the occasional rap of a cosmic ray or the more rapid, fainter, reports of radium numerals on the wristwatches of passing tourists.

"Keep close to the walls," Kinsey murmured. "Wolfram said he might conceal a pen behind something, especially around the doors near the offices or meeting room."

"I think we're on the wrong floor," she said. "Let's go up."

With other tourists they climbed to the main floor and soon found themselves strolling through the Senate's small rotunda. They peered through an open door into the old Senate chamber and then wandered toward the Senate meeting room.

A guard turned them back.

"At least there's no casual access to the important spots." Kinsey noted.

"And no logical place to put a pen."

They retraced their steps through the main rotunda into the House wing. In Statuary Hall they pretended to examine the names on the monuments as they skirted the perimeter. Then they moved in the direction of the House chambers. Kinsey tried the door of the House cloakroom, but it was locked. At that moment its guard reappeared from around the east corner.

"Sorry folks. It's closed to the public."

"Gee," said Kinsey. "We'd love to have a look."

"The House will be in session tomorrow. You can get a pass for the visitors' gallery. Come back then. More to see."

"Tomorrow," Kinsey muttered. "Tomorrow could be too late. Can we leave that way?" He pointed in the direction from which the guard had come.

"Sure. Right around the corner is the Grand Staircase. It'll lead you to ground level."

Kinsey took Juanita by the arm. "I guess we'd better move on to our next assignment. There's nothing here, not even a respectable click."

They strolled down the tile-floored hallway and turned into the staircase area. As they did a slim, intense-looking man with crew-cut hair hurried from the opposite direction.

"Is that area open to the public?" Kinsey asked the man as he passed them.

The man stopped adruptly and stared at each of them. "Open to the public? No, it is closed." He smiled. "Unless you have official papers to allow you in."

Juanita returned the smile. "No," she said. "We have nothing official."

They stared at each other for a moment. Then the blond man nodded, turned on his heel, and strode away toward the Senate wing.

By means mysterious and distressing to the constituted authorities, word came down to let Wolfram and his associates have whatever access they required for the White House and it environs.

Subsequently, he and Harada had spent the entire day touring all of the rooms of the Executive Mansion proper and some key outer offices, checking the official limousines, odd corners, and washrooms – to no avail. Their radiometers detected nothing but clock dials and electronic equipment, some official, some not.

Late in the afternoon they met in the main security office with Hamir and a duty officer. The Lebanese was plainly in acute distress. Wolfram urged him to return to the hospital.

"Absolutely not!" Hamir's face had the clammy sheen of trauma. The tight skin already hinted at death.

"As you wish," said Wolfram.

"What's your next move?" the duty officer asked.

"Obviously, our man has not yet planted any of the pens."

"And he won't," the duty officer said. "We've got this place bottled up. No unauthorized people get near here."

"What about authorized people?" Harada asked.

"What the hell's that supposed to mean?"

"What it means is that our man might have authorization." Wolfram glanced at Harada. "Thank you. We should have been working on that earlier."

The duty officer gaped at them in disbelief. "You've got to be kidding! Every single authorized individual has had top security clearance."

"Do you have their security files here?"

"Secret Service has them."

"Get 'em!"

"There are *hundreds.*"

"Get 'em!"

The duty officer picked up his telephone and dialed. A minute later, he cupped the mouthpiece and asked, "You want everybody or just certain categories?"

"We'll start with workmen, janitors, correspondents. If we don't find what we want, we'll ask for more."

The instructions were transmitted, and the duty officer hung up the receiver. "They'll be here in an hour."

Back in his motel room Jaeger began his preparations.

First, he unpacked a set of coveralls. Outwardly they had the appearance of better-tailored mechanic's togs. But their weight was unusual, for the front of them had an inner lining consisting of several layers of tungsten mesh. Jaeger stripped off his other clothes and donned the suit. Then he put on a hoodlike headpiece of the same material with a thick glass face place like a welder's mask.

Next, he assembled his tripod and lever arrangement. Beside it he placed a heavy-duty radiometer with a large dial.

Finally, he slipped on his gauntlets, lined with the same tungsten mesh, and began the difficult and delicate task of opening the steel

257

chest and inner tungsten container of radioactive material.

Painstakingly, using the clawed lever as a hand, he transferred the contents of the cylinder into his unusual camera, which lay next to the steel chest, its back open. After all the objects had been placed precisely inside the feed mechanism of the camera, he inserted several carbon dioxide cartridges and then closed the heavy back panel.

The radiometer gauge was on the high side, he noted, but not dangerously so. His total roentgen dosage should be inside the safety limits.

Now, he thought, to try it out once again. Deftly, he lifted the camera up onto the tripod, attached a remote control cord, and stepped back. He opened one of the room's windows and looked out. Across the river and Potomac Park the Capitol dome glowed with a pastel pink under the last rays of the dying day.

He stared at the spectacle for a moment and then went back to his work. Swinging the long bellows snout of the camera toward the open window, he flicked a safety switch and then triggered the remote control cord. There was a sharp click inside the box. A small, gleaming object whizzed past the window sash and out into the night.

Wolfram, Harada, and Hamir began combing the security clearance files. The procedure was simple, but slow. Wolfram examined the photographs inside each folder, glanced at the personal data, handed the folder to Hamir. He did the same and handed the material to Harada. Any photograph or information that remotely attracted their attention was put aside for closer examination.

They skimmed through the service personnel first and gleaned a dozen "possibles."

"Shall we give these a closer look or go on to the correspondents?" Wolfram asked Harada.

"Let's go on. I'm not satisfied that any of the ones we've picked could be our man."

Wolfram picked up a batch of the journalists' dossiers from the cart. A number of the folders had cryptic notes stapled to the jackets. He began scanning the folders and passing them along.

"What's this?" Wolfram asked, looking more carefully at one folder. "Great Rooms Project?"

The duty officer shook his head. "Can't quite recall – oh, yeah, I do. That's a photographer from some German art magazine coming in to take pictures of the White House architecture or something."

Wolfram opened the folder. The glossy photograph of a sharp-eyed Nordic type stared back at him. He passed the file to Hamir.

The Lebanese glanced at it, then looked again. "Familiar, somehow. I may have met him somewhere." He glanced at the written material in the file. "Heinz Jaeger," he read. He rummaged through the carbons of letters and forms. He stared at the picture and then handed it slowly to Harada.

"Wolfram," he whispered. "I think we have something here."

"Let me look again," said Hamir. He turned the picture as Harada had done. "I don't know. I don't know."

Wolfram retrieved the folder and glanced at the documents. "He's coming into the White House on Monday night. Tomorrow."

"The timing is right," said Hamir.

"Exactly," said Wolfram.

Harada turned to the duty officer. "Is there a photocopying machine here?"

"In the secretarial area." He motioned at the door to the next room.

Harada unclipped the photograph from the file and walked quickly with it into the adjacent area, the others on his heels. They turned on the copying machine and waited impatiently for its five-minute warm-up to end.

"The dossier fits," said Wolfram. "He's going into the Oval Office, the Blue Room. He'll be bringing large equipment. Perfect cover."

"The photography equipment could be made heavy enough to shield the pens," Hamir said. "He could drop them easily. Enough not only to kill, but *overkill.*"

"*One* pen is overkill. But why overkill?"

"More concentrated lethality, I'd guess," said Harada.

"But more dangerous for him, too," Wolfram replied. "And he couldn't just drop the pens on the floor or even conceal them too effectively. I wonder –"

He hurried back into the security office and grabbed the duty officer's telephone. In less than three minutes he tracked down his party at home.

"Dr. Atkinson?"

"Yes?"

"Wolfram here."

"We're in the middle of Sunday dinner, Mr. Wolfram. Could you call back in a half-hour?"

"I'm sorry, doctor, but it's quite urgent."

"What is it?"

"At our meeting the other day you told me that the cobalt pen weighed something over twelve grams."

"That's correct."

"And then you said that just a second or so of exposure to that much cobalt 60 would be fatal."

"Quite right. Twelve grams of cobalt 60 would have some two hundred times the energy of the same amount of radium."

"My question is this, how much cobalt 60 would produce a fatal dose of radiation in, let's say, two minutes?"

There was a pause at the other end of the line. "About a gram."

"How much would a gram of cobalt be? What could its appearance be?"

"In a spherical shape, for example, it would be about the size of a buckshot."

"Would that shape produce the optimum radiation?"

"It would depend on what you were trying to achieve."

"Suppose you were trying to create the most radiation from a shape, a surface."

"Something flat, then. A dime-size coin, perhaps." He paused. "Remember, this works like light. If you had a flat light bulb you'd get more illumination from the wide surfaces than from a round bulb of the same volume and wattage."

"Thank you, doctor."

"What's it all –?"

But Wolfram had hung up.

As he did, Harada and Hamir raced toward him with a photocopy of Heinz Jaeger's picture.

"See!" said Harada. "The contasts now are sharper, the eyebrows and lashes darker. Now" – he seized a pencil from the duty officer's desk – "we sketch in a beard and –" He held his hand across the cropped hair.

"It's *him!*" shouted Hamir.

22

Jaeger had called ahead. Consequently, when his van rolled up and parked opposite the House wing of the deserted Capitol, a uniformed officer awaited him. It was 9 P.M.

"Good evening," Jaeger said cheerfully as he climbed out of the driver's seat. His coveralls made his movements a bit awkward, but not so much that the unsuspecting would notice. "I hope it's okay, but I brought this young man along to help me porter my equipment."

A husky black youth climbed out of the rider's seat.

"He can help you carry the stuff up, but unless he has some papers, he'll have to wait outside. You know the red tape."

"No problem."

Standing back, Jaeger directed the unloading. The heavy bags stowed neatly on the hand truck. Jaeger himself carried the lighter bags.

With the guard leading the way, they went directly into the ground-floor area, up the Grand Staircase into the House peripheral rooms, and then up into the visitors' gallery. The going was somewhat difficult for the heavily laden hand truck, but Jaeger was patient.

They left the hand truck just outside the visitor's space, and Jaeger directed movement of the equipment to a position just behind the gold-framed clock above the Speaker's rostrum. The House was dimly illuminated by the high indirect lights in the ceiling.

"Will there be enough light in here for you? I can turn up the rheostat, if you want."

"No, this is fine," said Jaeger. "I'm going

to make long time exposures. Too much light could spoil the balance."

Jaeger told the young man how to set up the tripod.

"I'm paying this kid to save my back, so I might as well get my money's worth," he whispered to the guard.

"Right." The man watched the black youth struggle to lift the heavy camera. "That must be a heavy piece."

"Has to be for this kind of work," Jaeger assured him. "Even in here, you get vibrations that can affect lighter equipment. So I use heavy gear."

"Makes sense. When the boys are in session, you really get vibrations."

"I'll bet you do. When do they come back?"

"Tomorrow. Noon sharp the gavel falls."

"Do they usually all attend?"

"For the opening session of the week they do."

"Good."

"All set, Mr. Jaeger," the youth called.

"Swell. You go on back to the van then." He glanced at his watch. "Be back here in thirty minutes."

"Do you want me to stay with you?" the officer asked.

"Preferably not. You're a nice fellow and

I'd enjoy your company, but you might vibrate."

"Okay, then. I'll stand by and escort our friend here back up in a half-hour."

"Just right." Jaeger leaned forward confidentially. "This is dull work, really. Please close the door behind you. It'll shut out that extra light from the hallway."

As soon as the gallery door closed, he opened one of his carryall bags and extracted the strange hood and gauntlets and donned them. Then he moved to the camera.

Methodically, he aimed it at the furthest position in the rear tier of seats and began his work. The camera clicked and kept on clicking. Each time he moved it slightly to sight on a different point. In all, the mechanism triggered more than two hundred times before he was satisfied that he had covered every square yard of the House members' area.

For the Speaker's chair, the camera clicked twice.

He smiled with satisfaction. No one would notice those tiny, ordinary objects sytematically sprinkled around the chamber. The United States House of Representatives now was the most lethal room in the world.

It was 9:27 P.M. when Juanita and Kinsey rejoined the others in the White House security office.

"We toured it all," said Kinsey. "Capitol, House and Senate office buildings, Supreme Court."

"And we were chased by guards at all of them," Juanita added.

"We found nothing. Not a decent click, let alone a pen."

"No matter," said Wolfram. "It's finally dawned on me that he's using something other than pens, something smaller. It also looks like the White House is the target after all." He handed them Harada's photocopy with the pencilled-in beard. "We've identified our man. He'll be here late tomorrow night, unless the Secret Service and FBI have tracked him down before. They're on it now. Finally."

Kinsey frowned at the photocopy. "That's the emir?"

"That's the guy," said Hamir.

"How did you get this?"

"He's traveling incognito," said Wolfram, "as one Heinz Jaeger, who looks like this." Wolfram handed them the original photograph.

"Juanita!" Kinsey gasped.

"It's that man!" she cried.

"What man?" Wolfram demanded.

"Near the House of Representatives," said Kinsey. "He walked past us. I asked him a question."

"You're sure?"

"It's him!" Juanita exclaimed. "Those eyes!"

"My God," said Harada. "He may already have poisoned the place.

"He was empty-handed when we saw him," said Juanita. "Our radiometers made no sound."

Wolfram was already on the telephone to the Capitol police detail. After an agonizing delay, he reached the night commander. "On your docket, do you have a visit scheduled by anyone named Heinz Jaeger?"

"Yes. A photographer. What's the matter? Who *is* this?"

"Look," snapped Wolfram, "whatever you do, keep your men – everybody – away from the House and Senate chambers and offices! There is grave danger! Repeat. Grave danger!"

"What the hell is this? A bomb? Who are you?"

"This is a top security matter. I'll explain it to you when I get there. Five munutes. I'm calling from the White House."

"Wait a min –!"

268

"Don't argue. Have all of your people away from those wings. Outside, if possible. And you meet me in front of the House steps. Got it?"

"But –"

"Do it!"

Wolfram hung up sharply.

"Let's go!"

A Secret Service car with Wolfram driving careened out onto Pennsylvania Avenue and sped through red lights – followed by another car filled with Secret Service personnel – past the Justice Department and the Archives Building toward the Capitol.

In front of the House steps stood a cluster of uniformed men, the Capitol night force. Wolfram braked sharply and leaped out.

"What the hell is going on?" demanded the night commander as the second car screeched to a halt and agents exploded from it.

"Now listen to me and listen close," said Wolfram. "I'll only go through it once."

Quickly he sketched the situation for them.

"To sum it up, I'll go in alone, with this" – he held up Kinsey's radiometer – "and a gun." He looked around. *"Yours!"* he ordered a surprised Secret Service man.

"I can't just –"

"You want us all to go like *that*," Wolfram pointed at Hamir, who was leaning weakly against the car, his arms clutched across his cramping stomach. "He's dying from this bastard's poison. Now give me the pistol."

The Secret Service man handed him his Colt Detective Special.

"Now," said Wolfram, "the rest of you set up a cordon. Check out that van parked over there with Juanita's radiometer. Go!

"Kinsey, you call Dr. Atkinson of the Nuclear Energy Agency. He's at home. Tell him we need personnel and equipment here to handle a maximum radiation hazard."

"Got it."

"Okay. I'm going in."

Hamir staggered forward. "I'm going with you!"

"You've had it," Wolfram growled. "I'm sorry, but you're too sick."

Hamir's eyes were like coals, his face set in a grimace. "I *must*. I *must*." He clutched at Wolfram's arm.

Wolfram relented.

Together they entered on the ground level and slowly made their way up the Grand Staircase. Wolfram held the radiometer ahead of him like a talisman. At the top they followed the passageway along the House lobby. Wolfram singled out a key that fitted one of the doors. Silently, they entered the darkened room. A sliver of light glowed faintly beneath a door to the House chamber itself.

They moved toward it. Wolfram pushed it open with his radiometer. Instantly the device began to click frantically. He backed away quickly.

"The place is alive!" he whispered. "Stay back!"

"Let me go," said Hamir. "It can't hurt me anymore. Give me the counter."

He pushed the door inward. The counter roared. Hamir peered in and looked the chamber over carefully.

"Is he there?"

"He's gone!" He leaned down. "But here's his trail."

"Do you see any cobalt?"

Hamir leaned down in the dim light and picked something up. He waved it back and forth in front of the radiometer.

"What *is* it?"

Hamir turned and stared at him for a moment and then laughed bitterly. He hurled the tiny object aside.

"A *paper clip!* A goddamn cobalt-60 paper clip!"

At that moment the black youth finished setting up the camera on its tripod just to the left of the desk where the vice-president of the United States presided over the U.S. Senate.

"All set, Mr. Jaeger," he said, stepping aside.

"Here we go again, then. I'll be glad when it's over, and you'll probably be glad to have me out of your hair."

"Oh, no," the guard protested. "It's all very interesting. Breaks up the routine." He looked around. "The light okay in here? It seems brighter than in the House."

"It is, a little. No problem. I'll just stop the lens down a little." He moved toward his equipment. "See you fellows in a half-hour, then?"

After they left, Jaeger again donned his shielding garb. The tension of his task had abated as it became routine. Saturation would be more dense this time, he thought. One clip triggered for each of the one hundred seats, several for the podium, and the remainder fired randomly to exhaust what he thought of as his congressional ration. Even the subsequent cleanup by the service people wouldn't get all of the clips.

Allah is good to me, he thought.

Slowly he swung the camera around and aimed it at the farthest seat to his left.

Hamir was failing rapidly now. The exertion and nervous pressure of their efforts were taking a tremendous toll. As they made their way toward the Senate wing he twice doubled over with cramps and nearly fell. Wolfram held him tightly.

"Shall we stop and rest?" He had become well aware of Hamir's value at this point – a man who now had nothing to fear except a shortage of time.

"Keep going," Hamir gasped. "I'll make it."

Wolfram pulled the panting man's arm around his shoulder. "We can move faster this way."

"Do you think he'll be there?"

"I think so," Wolfram replied. "It'll be tight."

"You must be careful with your pistol. A bullet into his radioactive material could –"

The thought had crossed Wolfram's mind, too. A bullet shattering some radioactive source could create a penetrating dust that could never be eradicated.

"Where were the clips located, Hamir?"

"Scattered randomly, but uniformly, some on seats, some on the floor."

They were in the Senate wing now. "I think we should go up to the gallery," said Wolfram. "That'll give us the high ground and a clear view, and keep us away from the clips on the floor."

They found the steps to the visitor's gallery and went up silently. Hamir crawled from step to step. On the upper level, almost completely dark, they found a door. Wolfram nudged it open, radiometer at the ready. On hands and knees they slid through.

"Keep down," Wolfram whispered.

Gingerly, they crept behind the high wooden backs of the visitors' seats.

Wolfram ventured a quick look. There! He dropped back. "He's on the podium," he whispered. "He's wearing a coverall and some kind of hood with a face mask."

"What equipment?"

"Looks like a great big camera. On a heavy tripod."

He looked again. As he did the huge camera moved slightly. There was a faint plinking sound, and there was a dart of light across the chamber. It struck the leather back of one of the rear Senate chairs and fell back on the seat.

"We'll crawl around to the press gallery. That'll put us behind him. Maybe I can get a clean shot."

Hamir nodded faintly.

Agonizingly, they made their way until they were directly behind the podium. Their height cut off most of Wolfram's line of sight of the camera and man.

"Time to make our move." He rose, pulling the pistol from his pocket, and moved down through the tiers of the press gallery toward the edge. Hamir was beside him.

Halfway down Hamir staggered once again, bumping against one of the desks.

Below them the hooded head turned and looked up.

Wolfram raised his pistol and cocked it.

At the same instant, the figure swung the camera's snout around and ducked behind the heavy box.

"Don't shoot!" Hamir shouted. "Radiation!"

The camera snout tilted their way. For an instant action seemed to freeze, and then the ominous box fired. A paper clip struck a news desk not a foot from Wolfram and ricocheted back down to the Senate floor. The hooded figure wrestled the heavy equipment back to catch a higher angle on his target. Wolfram's radiometer made a tearing sound as gamma rays blended into a continuous stream.

Suddenly, beside Wolfram, Hamir

shrieked. He hurled himself forward, jostling Wolfram aside, bumping into the reporter's desks, and jarring them from their pedestals. He lurched toward the gallery rim just over the Senate clock.

"Hamir!"

A clip struck the Lebanese on the cheek and cut him. A trickle of blood rolled down his face.

"Come back, Hamir!"

The dying man vaulted over the edge and landed on the camera and the hooded man. All sprawled in a tangle across the step of the podium. The camera thudded loudly against the floor. Its backplate flew open and spewed clips on the carpeting.

Hamir clawed weakly at the hood of the man under him and pulled it away.

"Fool!" Jaeger screamed. "There's radiation!"

Frantically, he tried to roll out from under the jumble of equipment. Hamir clutched a handful of the spilled paper-clips and thrust them in the emir's grimacing face.

"Die! Die!"

The emir twisted madly. Clips fell inside the collar of his coveralls. With a convulsive push he rolled the equipment and the now-limp body of Hamir aside and leaped upright, tugging at the snaps of his coveralls.

The radiometer in Wolfram's hand crackled. Quickly, he backed upward into the gallery. Distance, he knew, was his only protection.

"Give it up!" he shouted. "You're dead!"

The Arab suddenly stopped and looked up at Wolfram, eyes burning.

"*You!*"

"Me – and *him!*"

Incredibly, a veil of calm fell across the emir's face. He turned and stared at Hamir. "And *he* is – was – an Arab." Then he looked back up at Wolfram.

"You're right, of course, I'm dead."

EPILOGUE

The cleanup was swift and expert. Congress met at noon, Monday, as scheduled.

The security agencies concocted a plausible cover story. A German photographer, mentally and mortally ill from a rare blood cancer, had attempted to plant bombs in the House and Senate wings of the Capitol. He had been readily apprehended and hospitalized.

The press gave this information cursory

attention. Deranged people were not uncommon around the Capitol. Nothing had exploded. Bomb-scare stories were clichés reported, best forgotten.

The man succumbed in his illness a week later. That drew a paragraph on the pity of it all in some journals, a somber passing line on newscasts.

Jaeger chose to die keeping his silence, but the domestic agencies retraced his route along the coast without too much difficulty.

They watched a Florida marina operator develop an anemia that puzzled his doctors, but from which he finally recovered. A similar thing happened to the motel workers in West Palm Beach and Rocky Mount, North Carolina. (Wolfram, of course, underwent extensive tests to determine what effect, if any, his exposure had had, but since he had never been closer than twenty feet to Jaeger, there were no ill effects, immediate or long-range.)

The black youth who had helped with the camera equipment was detained in his own home in Virgina as a material witness in the "bomb" case. The government paid his subsistence, of course. Eight days later he became ill, developed pneumonia, and died.

Coincidence.

Aside from those unfortunate events, the episode was a windfall all around.

For its part, the State Department was handed sure and powerful leverage in the oil-producing emirate of Al Hakeer. Despite a certain confusion of leadership there, loans were arranged to rebuild the oil depot on the Isle of Ishbaad in return for long-range guarantees of shipments of crude product at a reasonable price.

The Bank got the gold.

The Bank's man got a burial at public expense.